Lewis B. Monroe

Story of our Country

Lewis B. Monroe

Story of our Country

ISBN/EAN: 9783337227630

Printed in Europe, USA, Canada, Australia, Japan

Cover: Foto ©Andreas Hilbeck / pixelio.de

More available books at **www.hansebooks.com**

Pocahontas and her Attendants bringing Corn to the Settlement.
(See page 71.)

THE

STORY OF OUR COUNTRY.

BY

MRS. LEWIS B. MONROE.

BOSTON:

LEE AND SHEPARD, PUBLISHERS.

NEW YORK: CHARLES T. DILLINGHAM.

1880.

"*The greatest glory of a free-born people*
Is to transmit that freedom to their children."

Electrotyped at the
Boston Stereotype Foundry.
1º Spring Lane.

Copyright by
LOCKWOOD, BROOKS, & CO.,
1876.

Cambridge: Presswork by John Wilson and Son.

HINT TO TEACHERS.

The "STORY OF OUR COUNTRY" having found favor with the little ones for whom it was written, the writer is encouraged to say that it has been sucessfully used as a reading-book, meeting the wants of children using the Third or Fourth Reader of any series. A pleasant and profitable exercise is to let the children take turns in personating the characters of the dialogue, while the rest of the class find on their maps the places mentioned. Used in this way there need be only four books to a class;—one for the teacher, three for the children reading.

Mrs. L. B. MONROE.

November 12, 1879.

HOW THIS STORY CAME TO BE WRITTEN.

Mother and her two children, Will and Lizzie, are sitting before a bright fire in a pleasant parlor. Will is twelve years old and Lizzie ten. They are earnest, wide-awake children, full of fun and frolic; but through all their good times, they are constantly learning much that will be useful to them in after life. Mother never refuses to answer their ques-

tions; but with patient love seeks to impart to them
the desire of finding beauty and goodness everywhere.

What merry times, then, do **Will and Lizzie** have,
when, supper being over, they sit down before the
crackling logs in the open fireplace, to talk over the
pleasures of the day, or hear mother tell stories.

Ah! what stories has she told them!—of birds,
and beasts, and flowers! The wonders of fairy
land, too, she has often unfolded to the eager little
listeners. After **every** story, whether of child-life,
bird-life, or fairy-land, she is greeted by the question, "Is it true, mother?"

The delight with which Will and Lizzie always
hear the answer, "Yes, it is all true!" has led
mother to tell them

THE STORY OF OUR COUNTRY.

CONTENTS.

COLUMBUS.

KING PHILIP.

BENJAMIN FRANKLIN.

THE ACADIANS.

GEORGE WASHINGTON.

MARION.

BENEDICT ARNOLD.

THE STORY OF OUR COUNTRY.

I.

FOUR HUNDRED YEARS AGO.

MOTHER. — If we could be up in a balloon high enough to see the world beneath us, how do you think it would look?

WILL. — Like a great ball, of course.

MOTHER. — Now, if we could imagine ourselves to be living four hundred years ago, and up in a balloon, we should see very many more people on one side of the globe than on the other. We should find crowds of people in Europe, Asia, and the northern part of Africa; but we should find very few people on the other side of the globe; that is, in North and South America.

LIZZIE. — What should we see in America?

MOTHER. — We should see great forests and vast plains, or prairies. These prairies were covered with waving grass and beautiful flowers. Herds of buffaloes were sporting here. We should see, too, beautiful lakes and rivers, and troops of deer feeding along their banks. In the dark forests we should see foxes, wolves, and panthers.

LIZZIE. — Were there any bears?

MOTHER. — Yes, there were bears, and other wild animals; for there were so few people in America then that the animals were not driven from their wild haunts.

But let us see! If we had lived four hundred years ago, we should have known nothing about balloons; we should not have known even that the world was round.

WILL. — Why, mother, you do not mean to say that people were so stupid as not to know that the world is round!

MOTHER. — I do, indeed. For hundreds of years people had wondered what shape the earth could be. It was generally thought to be flat. In the fifteenth century there were many in every country of Europe who thought that the world *might be* round, and, if it were round, that there might be countries on the other side which they had never heard about.

WILL. — I don't see why captains and sailors had never come to other lands when they were cruising about.

MOTHER. — Ships were not built so strong in those days as they are now. Navigators — that is, people who follow the sea — had never dared to sail very far from the land. So they discovered only a few islands in their voyages.

England was a great power even then, and owned many ships. These ships sometimes went to Holland, or, still farther, to Russia, through the Baltic Sea. They oftener went south, along the western

Ships of the Fifteenth Century.

coast of France, and through the Straits of Gibraltar, into the Mediterranean Sea. A few ships had ventured still farther south, cruising along the western coast of Africa. But they had never gone far enough to learn the shape of Africa. Still less did they imagine that they might go around its southern point, and thus find a passage by water to the great countries of Asia.

WILL. — I tell you what! If I had been a navigator in those days, guess I would not have been afraid to cruise along till I found out the way to Asia!

MOTHER. — And if you had been such a brave navigator, Will, as to have dared to double the Cape of Good Hope, America might not have been discovered to-day.

LIZZIE. — Why, mother! I don't see how that could be.

MOTHER. — You know I told you just now that most of the ships went into the Mediterranean. The reason was, that all the countries of Europe carried on trade with India, the richest country of Asia. But it took a long time to get anything to or from that distant place ; for, after the ships had reached the eastern ports of the Mediterranean, then all the merchandise had to be carried to the Red Sea on the backs of camels. There the goods were again shipped for India. This was a very expensive way of trading; and in every country the merchants were saying, "Is there no easier way to get to India?"

About this time there was a little child born in Genoa, Italy. His grandfather and many of his

Loaded Camel.

uncles had followed the sea. As this little boy, whose name was Christopher, grew older —

WILL. — Do you mean Christopher Columbus?

MOTHER. — Yes, I am talking about Christopher Columbus when he was a little boy; and I began to say that when his uncles were home from sea, he heard them tell wonderful stories about the great ocean. He used to wish he were a man, so that he could go to sea, too. And, sure enough, when he became older, he did go, and made many voyages between the different ports in the Mediterranean Sea. Wherever he went, he always tried to learn something new. He was never ashamed to ask questions of those who were older than himself, or of those who had seen more of the world. And as he was so often at the large cities where the merchants were receiving goods from the East, he, of course, heard a great deal about a shorter passage to India.

At one time it so happened that the ship in which Columbus was sailing took fire. Columbus leaped overboard, and by the aid of an oar, which was floating in the water, he swam to the shore, a distance of six miles.

WILL. — Six miles! I say, not many men could swim six miles. Was he all alone then on an island, like Robinson Crusoe?

MOTHER. — No; he found himself in Portugal. He had a brother at Lisbon, the capital of Portugal. This brother, named Bartolomeo, earned his living by making maps and charts. Columbus went to see him.

After this, Columbus married the daughter of a sea captain. His wife's father owned a great many charts and nautical instruments, such as Columbus had never seen; so that he had a chance to learn still more about the sea.

LIZZIE. — But, mother, what did Columbus do for a living in Portugal?

MOTHER. — He made maps and charts. Then, too, he often went on voyages to Africa. When far out at sea, he would lie on the deck watching the stars, and thinking of Him who made them. He wondered if the stars were worlds. Then he thought of our own world, and wondered if it were round or flat. "If it is round," said he, "then we

might reach India by sailing west. Everybody
says that all Europe needs a shorter passage to
India. When men needed to venture on the seas
farther than they had before dared to do, did not
God give them the compass, to tell them which
way they were going? And will He not show
men the shorter route to India, if the time has
come when they need it? If the earth were
round, we could sail about it, and carry what is good
and useful in one country to all other countries.
Thus mankind would be made wiser, better, and
happier, if they could be sure that the world is
round. I *know* it must be round."

After this, Columbus never doubted that if he
were to sail west from Europe, he should come to
India. The thought haunted him so, day and night,
that he determined to see if he could not get his
government to fit out some vessels for a voyage
of discovery. "If there are new lands discovered,"
he said, "the flag of my native country shall be the
first to float over them." So he went to Genoa and
asked for aid. It was refused him, and he was
laughed at for his folly.

Then he got permission to go before the King
of Portugal. He showed the king his charts, and
explained to him why he believed the earth was
round.

WILL. — I hope this king was sensible, and let him have some ships.

MOTHER. — No; on the contrary, the king said, "The man is mad! Hasn't everybody always believed that the world was flat? And does this poor fellow know more than everybody else?"

WILL. — "Poor fellow!" Humph! He knew more than the king!

MOTHER. — Columbus was somewhat discouraged by the king's refusal, and for a time he felt that perhaps God had not chosen him to show people that the earth was round. His good wife died, too; and he was left all alone in the world with his little boy, Diego, whom he took with him wherever he went.

"I will leave Portugal, and go to Spain," he said. So he started on foot, with little Diego by his side, to travel to that country. He had spent what little money he had while trying to get a hearing with the King of Portugal. He was hungry, tired, and foot-sore, and was anxious about little Diego.

LIZZIE. — I know good Columbus cared more for his little boy than he did for himself.

MOTHER. — I think so, too; and he must have said to himself, "Will God let my little boy die with hunger?" · But at last he came to a monastery, where some good men lived who took pleasure in caring for tired travellers.

One of these men, Juan Perez, took pity on Columbus. He said, "This noble-looking man is no common beggar!" He not only gave him and his little boy food, clothing, and shelter, but he became the best friend Columbus had ever known. Of course Columbus told him all his history, and

Columbus with Diego begging at the Monastery.

how sure he was that he could find India, if he could only have vessels enough. He also told him how the King of Portugal had refused to aid him.

Juan Perez said, "How do you know but that our good King Ferdinand and his noble Queen Isabella may be willing to listen to you?"

2

"But," said Columbus, "I have no one to help me get a hearing at their court."

Juan Perez talked over the grand scheme of Columbus with the wisest navigators he knew. And when he found they believed that Columbus was right, he made up his mind that he would see what he himself could do to introduce Columbus to the king and queen. Now, it so happened that Juan Perez was a minister, or priest; and at one time the queen had sent for him, to talk with her about heavenly things. So he was not a stranger to the queen. He wrote a letter to Isabella, begging her to let him come and see her.

She consented; and Perez told her all about Columbus, — how noble and good he was, — and then asked her if his friend might come and tell his story for himself.

LIZZIE. — O, I hope Isabella let him come!

MOTHER. — Yes; Columbus was allowed to go before the king and queen, and tell what great things he hoped to do for the world.

King Ferdinand was not very friendly to Columbus; and said there was no money to spare for such an enterprise. But Isabella believed in him, and said, "He shall have the money, even if I have to part with all my jewels!"

WILL. — Good for Isabella! She thought more

of helping Columbus than she did of making a great show with her jewels.

MOTHER. — Isabella was worthy of being a queen, for she was always doing good. But she little thought how much good she was doing, when she gave orders to have vessels fitted out for Columbus.

WILL. — I guess that made Columbus a happy man!

MOTHER. — Yes, indeed. For ten years he had been trying to get help from the different governments.

LIZZIE. — Ten years! Poor man! I wonder he did not get discouraged.

MOTHER. — Great men are not easily discouraged.

II.

A BRAVE VOYAGE, AND WHAT CAME OF IT.

WILL. — I want to know whether little Diego went with his father on his great voyage.

MOTHER. — No; Diego was a little boy no longer. He was now twenty years old. The queen felt so kindly towards Columbus that she asked him if he would allow Diego to become a page to her little boy. Of course Columbus was very grateful to Isabella for this; for it was a great honor to Diego to have the king and queen trust the little prince with him.

WILL. — If I had been Diego, I should much rather have gone to sea with my father, than to have staid in the king's palace all the time.

MOTHER. — Diego may have felt so, too; but probably Columbus thought it would be for his son's advantage to have such good friends as the King and Queen of Spain might be to him.

So he bade good-by to Diego, and went to Palos, on the western coast of Spain, to oversee the fitting up of his ships.

WILL. — How many did he have? '

MOTHER. — Three; one large and two smaller ones. It took three months to get them ready to sail; for they stowed away provisions enough to last a whole year; and it was difficult to find sailors who were willing to start off on such an uncertain enterprise. " If we go, we shall never come back," they said.

But finally the crews were found, and the ships were ready to start.

WILL. — Of course Columbus went in the largest ship — didn't he?

MOTHER. — Yes; he took command of the Santa Maria. And one Friday morning in August, 1492, Columbus and his officers, having first asked God to bless and guide them, set sail, directing their course west from Spain.

When night came on, and they lost sight of land, they began to realize what dangers were before them.

" What fools we were to come ! " said the sailors. " Here we are, sailing off into the darkness, we know not where. Even Columbus himself does not know ! "

But the next morning, when the bright sun rose over the waters, they felt less afraid, and said, " Perhaps we may find a wonderful country."

After they had been sailing about five weeks,

they saw a large tree or mast floating on the water. This gave them all new hope, and they said, " We shall surely see land soon."

But in two weeks after this, a fearful storm came on, which terrified the crews so much that they said, " God is not pleased with us. Columbus must turn back.' But the storm cleared away, and soon after this, all on board the ships were thrilled with joy as they heard the cry, " Land! land!"

LIZZIE. — O, mother!

WILL. — Guess the sailors did not think they had been fools then!

MOTHER. — Columbus was so overjoyed that he caused the anthem, " Glory to God in the highest!" to be sung in all the ships.

But, alas! as they drew near the supposed land, it proved to be only a thick cloud in the horizon.

After this, the sailors were more discouraged than ever. " Shall a hundred and twenty of us throw away our lives for the sake of one man who has lost his senses?" said they. " No! let us seize Columbus, and throw him overboard!"

But Columbus was not afraid of the men. He went amongst them, and said, " My brave men, I *know* we are coming to a glorious land — a land where we may find more beautiful treasures than we ever dreamed of. Shall we all turn cowards?

What immortal honor will that sailor have who first spies land! And if honor be not enough for him, then shall he have a purse of gold."

Arrival of Columbus's Fleet.

This gave the sailors fresh hope and courage. And at two o'clock in the morning, October 12, seventy-one days after they had left Spain, they were again all startled with joy. A gun was fired from one of the ships, and they heard the cry, "Land! land! land!"

As soon as the light enabled them to see, they found themselves near a beautiful island. The air was filled with a delicious fragrance from unknown flowers. They saw trees laden with fruit, such as they had never seen before. Strange, bright birds were flitting in and out of the shady groves.

Columbus and all his men were enchanted. "One would like to live in a place like this forever," said they.

Soon they saw crowds of half-clothed natives running along the shore.

"Who are those people?" asked the sailors of Columbus.

"They must be Indians," said he. For Columbus thought they had reached India.

WILL. — Well, there! now I know why the red men of America are called Indians.

MOTHER. — Yes, Columbus thought he had at last got an answer to the merchants' question, "How shall we find an easier passage to India?"

LIZZIE. — But he was not quite right — was he, mother?

MOTHER. — No; and probably he himself knew that he had not reached the *trading* part of India. He evidently thought he had found a portion of India that was unclaimed by any sovereign. For, with his heart full of gratitude to Isabella, without whose favor he never could have made the great discovery, he was anxious to claim the new-found land for her. So, as soon as the morning sun gilded the eastern waters, boats were lowered from the ships. Then, midst the sound of martial music and the firing of guns, the three commanders were rowed to land.

Columbus first stepped on the beach. Filled with awe and gratitude to God, he stooped and kissed the ground, wetting it with his tears. Then, rising and drawing his sword, he unfurled the royal banner, and took possession of the new-found land in the name of the crown of Spain.

LIZZIE. — O, how thankful Ferdinand and Isabella must have been to Columbus!

WILL. — I want to know what the natives did. Were they afraid?

MOTHER. — No; when they saw the ships, they supposed them to be great birds coming to them from Heaven.

LIZZIE. — They must have thought the sails were the birds' wings.

MOTHER. — And when they saw Columbus and his officers step on shore, they thought they were gods. They bowed themselves to the ground. They kissed Columbus's feet. Then they brought the best of everything they had to the new comers.

WILL. — What did they bring?

MOTHER. — They brought beautiful flowers; and gave them bananas and honeycomb to eat. They spread fresh palm-leaves on the ground for them to lie down on. They made their little children come and kiss them. They showed them beautiful springs of water. Then they invited them by signs to their little houses, which were huts or wigwams. In short, these poor, simple natives did everything in their power to show that they were glad to see the strangers.

LIZZIE. — I hope Columbus treated them well.

MOTHER. — Yes. One day a sailor was unkind to one of the natives. Columbus was very angry. He invited the Indian on board his ship, and gave him beads and other trinkets. Then he let him go back to the shore. The sailors watched him through a spy-glass, to see what he would do.

WILL. — What did he do?

MOTHER. — He put on all the finery which Columbus had given him. Then he strutted up and down the shore, to show himself off to the other natives.

Now look on your maps, and find where Columbus first landed. He called the island San Salvador.

WILL. — Why, that is in the mouth of the Gulf of Mexico — one of the West Indies — isn't it?

MOTHER. — Yes; and can you not tell now, Lizzie, why those islands are called the West *Indies?*

LIZZIE. -- O, I see! Columbus thought at first he had found India.

The Voyage of Columbus.

MOTHER. — Yes; and India is sometimes called the East Indies.

LIZZIE. — And the country Columbus found by sailing west from Spain they called the *West Indies.*

MOTHER. — You are quite right. Look once more on the map, and find the other islands discovered by Columbus. They are Conception, Ferdinand and Isabella, Exuma, Cuba, and Hayti. He must have liked the looks of Hayti, for when he reached here, he took to pieces his largest ship, the Santa Maria, and built a fort, calling the island Hispaniola, or Little Spain.

He cruised about the islands for three months, and then went back to Spain, taking some of the natives with him.

III.

WHAT AFTERWARDS HAPPENED TO COLUMBUS.

WILL. — We want to hear more about Columbus, and how he was treated when he got back to Spain.

MOTHER. — I wish I could tell you as delightful things about his life as you heard in our last talk; but I must tell you the truth, though it is not always pleasant to hear.

When Columbus first reached Spain, ten weeks after he left Hayti, or Hispaniola, he was received with a great deal of attention. The king and queen and all the court people heard him tell his adventures with as much interest as you listen to me. The king appointed him governor of Hispaniola, and placed him in command of seventeen ships and fifteen hundred men, to go back and make other discoveries. His brother Bartolomeo went with him.

LIZZIE. — I am sure, mother, he had good luck.

MOTHER. — So he had, up to this point; but after this everything seemed to go against him. It was not so easy for Columbus to manage fifteen hundred men as one hundred and twenty. Many of the men were envious because they had never made great discoveries. Then, too, they thought they should find gold and precious stones lying about on the ground as common as pebbles; because they saw that the natives whom Columbus brought back wore rich jewels on their necks.

WILL. — They were not very bright to think so, any how. They might have known that the Indians wouldn't care anything about gold, if it was as plenty as dust. They wouldn't think any more of it than they would of common stones in the street.

MOTHER. — You are perfectly right, Will. And you will always find that men value things just in proportion as the things are hard to get. But these foolish men did not think of this. They wanted to become rich without working; and because they found they could not do this, they hated Columbus, and said he was a traitor and a liar. They even tried to take his life.

WILL. — Then they were meaner than the sailors who wanted to throw him overboard; for they were afraid for their own lives. But these men were already in the beautiful new country.

MOTHER. — Yes, Will; and when Columbus, after trying for three years, found it was impossible to satisfy them in any way, he made up his mind to go back to Spain, first having discovered the Windward Islands, Jamaica, and Porto Rico. He also founded a colony in Hispaniola, and left it in command of his brother Bartolomeo.

LIZZIE. — Wasn't the king glad to see Columbus this time?

MOTHER. — Not so glad as before. The men who returned with him said untrue things about him. And then, too, the king expected he would have made greater discoveries on this voyage than on the first.

WILL. — Perhaps Ferdinand thought that as he let him have ten times as many men, he ought to have discovered just so many more new countries to pay for it.

MOTHER. — Perhaps so. The king does not seem to have lost confidence in him entirely, though his coolness hurt Columbus very much. Isabella still believed in him; and it was through her influence that money was raised for another voyage.

He remained in Spain about two years, and then returned across the Atlantic, this time with six ships. Instead of going directly back to the West Indies, he bore farther south, till he reached the mouth of the Orinoco.

LIZZIE. — I remember that river. It is in South America.

MOTHER. — Yes. And when Columbus saw what a wonderful river it was, and what beautiful flowers and magnificent trees grew along its banks, and what bright-plumed birds were in the trees, he said, "This must be the river that flows through the Garden of Eden!"

His health was then very poor; so he went to Hispaniola to rest. But the poor man had anything but rest there. He found great confusion on the island. Every one wanted to please himself, and would not mind Bartolomeo, who was lieutenant governor in Columbus's absence.

King Ferdinand heard of the troubles in Hispaniola, and sent over an officer to inquire into affairs there. But the officer, before making any inquiries, arrested Columbus and his brother, and put them in chains.

LIZZIE. — O, how cruel!

MOTHER. — Columbus was thrown into prison, where he was confined many weary months.

One day he asked of an officer who came to lead him from his cell, "Are you taking me to death?"

"Your excellency is to be conducted to Spain," was the answer.

WILL. — Columbus taken to Spain!

MOTHER. — Yes, and in chains. The officers on board the ship were ashamed of the insults heaped upon him. They felt their own littleness in the presence of this brave discoverer — this greatest man of the age. They offered to free him from his chains. But Columbus said, sadly and proudly, —

"No! I will wear them as a memento of the gratitude of princes!"

LIZZIE. — But, mother, what was the king thinking of? Columbus on this voyage had discovered the continent of South America.

MOTHER. — The king seems to have thought little of this. It is true that when Columbus arrived in Spain, the king gave orders to have him immediately released. But Ferdinand was dissatisfied, and appointed another man governor of Hispaniola.

LIZZIE. — Didn't Isabella do something for Columbus then?

MOTHER. — The noble queen never lost faith in him; and when she first saw him after his arrest, she felt so much pity for him that she wept.

WILL. — I believe in Isabella!

MOTHER. — Her generous sympathy did much towards reviving the courage of Columbus. She again fitted him out for a voyage at her own expense, taking money which she had intended to use at the wedding of her daughter Isabella. And Columbus started off on his third voyage.

This time he was in command of only four ships

and one hundred and fifty men. His object was to search for a passage through the Gulf of Mexico. He stopped at Hispaniola, but was refused admission to the island. After cruising about for two years on the south coast of the gulf, he was driven by famine and other hardships back to Spain.

Isabella, his best friend, was dead. He was now seventy years old, poor, and out of health. He had no home to go to, and had scarcely money enough to pay for a lodging.

"The king knows it all, but does not care," he said to himself.

But through all his misfortunes, Columbus never lost his trust in God.

"Into thy hands, O Lord, do I commit my spirit," were his last words.

Thus this greatest of discoverers died in poverty, and almost alone. For a long time scarcely any one knew where his body was laid. But after seven years the king felt ashamed not to have noticed his death. So he caused a marble tomb to be erected over his remains, with the words inscribed upon it, "To CASTILE AND LEON COLUMBUS GAVE A NEW WORLD."

LIZZIE. — Doesn't Spain own very much land in America now?

WILL. — Not much, and I am glad of it.

MOTHER. — No; Spain now owns but two of the West India islands, though she formerly owned a large part of South America. Will says he is glad Spain does not own much on this continent, since, through her ingratitude to Columbus, she threw away her chance of owning the whole of it, or at least of laying claim to it.

I am glad, too, that Spain did not get a stronger foothold on this continent; but not for the same reasons as yours, Will. If the Spaniards had ruled here, we, the descendants of the Puritans, might not have enjoyed such privileges as we now enjoy.

At another time I shall tell you how the other countries of Europe began to lay claim to American soil. Before we close this talk, you will be interested to know that the remains of Columbus having been twice removed from their resting-place, were finally conveyed with great pomp to the cathedral of Havana, where they now repose.

WILL. — I want to know why our country was n't named after Columbus. It seems to me that it ought to have been.

MOTHER. — It does seem so; and the poet must have thought so when he wrote, —

"Hail, Columbia, happy land!"

This country was called America in honor of

Americus Vespucius, who sailed across the ocean seven years after Columbus's great discoveries.

WILL. — I don't think it was fair, to honor Americus Vespucius more than Columbus. It was no great feat to follow in another man's footsteps.

MOTHER. — So I think. All the world knows that Columbus was the greater hero of the two.

LIZZIE. — Mother, I want to know what became of Diego. Was he alive when Columbus died?

MOTHER. — Yes. He afterwards claimed from the king the rights that had been granted and then taken from his father. He thus became Governor of Hispaniola. He soon after married the daughter of a duke. He seems to have had a quiet life, quite unlike the daring, enterprising life his father had lived.

IV.

MORE DISCOVERIES.

Mother. — We have seen that Spain was the first European country that laid claim to the lands this side of the Atlantic. But while the Spanish flag was flying in the West Indies, the kings of the other countries in Europe were saying, "Would that Columbus had been a subject of ours!"

Will. — I wonder if Columbus would have met with no better luck, if he had done as much for some other king.

Mother. — We cannot know that; but I do know that the next adventurer who went across the sea to claim land for his king, died also a poor, forgotten man.

Lizzie. — Why, mother, who was that?

Mother. — His name was John Cabot. He, too, was born in Italy, but he had gone to live in England. As Columbus had proved that the world was round, it was not difficult for John Cabot to get leave of the King of England to go across the seas to discover other new lands.

"Columbus did not find the main land of India—only the islands this side of it," said Cabot. "Who knows but that I can discover the trading part of India!"

So John Cabot and his three sons, in the year 1497, started off in a single vessel to try their fortunes in the western world. After they had been sailing a month, they reached the northern part of the continent of North America.

LIZZIE. — In 1497? Why, that was one year before Columbus discovered South America.

WILL. — But five years after he had proved that there was land across the water.

MOTHER. — The Cabots really discovered the main land of America before Columbus did. But I feel we must give all the honor to Columbus. Later discoverers were cheered on by what they knew had been done by other men. Columbus, calm and brave, relied only on the voice of God in his own heart.

WILL. — Did the Cabots stay long on the continent?

MOTHER. — No, they did not. They sailed along the coast far enough to be convinced that they had found a continent; then, as they were getting short of provisions, they returned to England.

"We did not find India," they said to the king; "but we think we found China."

This pleased the English king, Henry VII., very much; and he said, "Go back again with six large ships, and find other lands."

But John Cabot died soon after this. So the

Cabot's Ships among the Icebergs.

most enterprising of his sons, Sebastian Cabot, made the voyage.

"We shall surely now find the shorter passage to India," said Henry VII.

Sebastian Cabot sailed to the far north, enduring great hardships amongst the icebergs. Then he sailed along the coast as far south as Florida. He landed upon the continent in several places, and planted the English flag.

"This is the most immense country the world ever dreamed of!" said Sebastian.

WILL. — It seems to me Sebastian Cabot must have had a strange sort of feeling when he was putting those flags along the coast. Just think! All that great country, and no white man ever there before!

LIZZIE. — Don't you believe he was afraid?

WILL. — Afraid? No! What was there to be afraid of? Only wild animals. And of course his gun would keep those off. I know what I should have kept thinking, if I had been Sebastian Cabot.

MOTHER. — Well, what?

WILL. — I should have said to myself, "What will Henry VII. say when I get back to England, and tell him of this great country?"

MOTHER. — When Henry VII. was told that Sebastian had not found India, he was vexed, and said, "The voyage was a failure."

WILL. — I didn't know before that kings could be so stupid.

MOTHER. — One reason why the English king was

disappointed, was because Portugal had become famous in discoveries through Vasco da Gama. This man, fitted out by the Portuguese government, had reached India by the Cape of Good Hope. And all Europe was rejoicing that the passage to India by water had been found.

LIZZIE. — Didn't Sebastian Cabot fare any better than Columbus?

MOTHER. — Not in the treatment he received from Henry VII. Upon that king's death, Sebastian was called to Spain by Ferdinand.

WILL. — Ah, ha! I guess Ferdinand began to think he had n't made out of Columbus all that he might have done.

MOTHER. — Perhaps so. At any rate, he always treated Sebastian Cabot with honor. He made him Pilot Major of Spain; and no ship was allowed to sail to the West Indies that Cabot had not examined and approved.

LIZZIE. — Didn't Sebastian Cabot ever go to America again?

MOTHER. — Yes; his voyage was not a very successful one, however.

Sebastian Cabot was second only to Columbus among the many adventurers who crossed the Atlantic. He braved dangers and hardships not for his own sake. Like Columbus, he hoped thereby to benefit the world. He lived to be an old man; but to the last he was full of enthusiasm about the new-found world.

In the latter part of his life he returned to England. Queen Mary was then upon the throne. Under her patronage a party of discoverers were about to start off for America. Sebastian Cabot rejoiced at this almost as much as if he were going himself.

"I am too old to go," he said. "I may not live to hear you tell your adventures. But my heart goes with you."

On the eve of their sailing he went on board their ship, and gave each one of the crew a handsome sum of money. Then, going on shore, he invited the whole ship's company to a supper. After the supper they had a dance; and the dear old man, then eighty-one years old, got up and joined in the merry-making. His heart grew young at the thought that other men might make still greater discoveries than he had done.

WILL. — He was better off than Columbus; for *he* had no money to treat his friends with, if he had wanted to.

MOTHER. — True. Queen Mary provided Sebastian Cabot with a comfortable living. But England did not then realize all that he had done. Her queens and kings, however little they may have done, are mouldering to-day under gorgeous monuments; but no one knows the burial-place of him who gave England a continent.

WILL. — I should think every king in Europe would have wanted to own land in America. Didn't any other kings send ships over to make discoveries?

MOTHER. — The King of France was the next to lay claim to a part of the continent. Seven years after the discoveries by the Cabots, a number of humble fishermen from the northern part of France went to Newfoundland, and established a successful fishing trade. And thirty-seven years after the English flags were planted on the coast, the French flag was flying over the country we now call Canada.

LIZZIE. — Then there were only three kings owning land in America.

MOTHER. — True; the kings of England, France, and Spain. For a number of years after the time we are now talking of, France owned Canada. England owned the country along the coast, and for some distance inland, between Canada and Florida. Spain claimed the West Indies, and all the country around the Gulf of Mexico.

WILL. — It must have been good fun to go over

to a new country and explore, and see what one could find. I suppose that is how America got to be so full of people afterwards. I should have liked it, I tell you!—to follow up the rivers that you knew were not on the maps, and climb the mountains, to see what kind of a country it was! And then I should like to hunt for gold and precious stones, and get acquainted with the Indians.

MOTHER. — Ah, my boy! you little know the hardships one has to suffer in going to a new country! I shall try to give you an idea of it in telling you of the first settlements.

LIZZIE. — Well, mother, did the people go over to America because they thought they would like there just what Will says he would like?

MOTHER. — There seem to have been three different reasons why people went over from Europe to America. Columbus and several navigators after him went to find a western passage to the East Indies. When a passage had been found to India by going around Africa, then the cry was, "Let us go to America for gold!"

But it is a singular fact that no comfortable homes were established in America till people went — not for discovery, not for gold, but for freedom — freedom to have such governments as the people needed, and freedom to worship God.

LIZZIE. — Didn't the people have freedom in Europe?

MOTHER. — They did not have such freedom as we have in this country. Only kings and nobles were rich there; they lived lives of ease, and were sup-ported by the poor people, who had to work hard all the time, and then did not have enough to eat.

WILL. — What! these poor people had to give their money to the rich? I would not stand that!

MOTHER. — That is the way kings have been sup-ported. But when people heard that there was a beautiful great country across the waters, they be-gan to say, "Wouldn't it be better to go and try our fortunes there, rather than to stay here, where we know we shall be poor and half starved all our days?" So America began to grow.

Crossing the Ocean.

V.

TRYING TO MAKE HOMES IN AMERICA.

MOTHER. — About one hundred years after America was discovered, there was a very wise queen on the throne of England, whose name was Elizabeth. She seemed always anxious to do what seemed for the glory of her country. She had thought a great deal about America. She said to herself, "Who knows but these lands in America may bring wealth to my people?" So when one of her favorites, Sir Walter Raleigh — handsome, kind, and brave Sir Walter Raleigh — asked if he might try to make homes for the English people in America, Elizabeth was very glad. She gave him the privilege of fitting out ships, and sending such things as were needed to make people comfortable in their new homes.

Raleigh loved and honored his queen. For her sake he was anxious to do everything in his power for the good of England. This is one reason why he was interested in settling America. He said, "America would be a precious jewel in the crown of our queen, if it could be settled and made prosperous by her English subjects. I will work for this. I will use my money to fit out ships. I will do all I can to attract people to America."

Raleigh before Queen Elizabeth.

And Sir Walter Raleigh had more to do with colonizing this country than any other man. Still, all the settlements made by the people he sent over were failures.

WILL. — I don't see why, if they had provisions — that is, if they did not go too far north.

MOTHER. — They did not go too far north, nor too

far south. They landed in a pleasant season of the
year. But one great cause of their troubles was,
that they were not kind to the natives. At one
time these first settlers came to a little Indian
town. They missed a silver cup. Of course they
knew some Indian had taken it. And what do you
suppose the white people did in return?

LIZZIE. — I guess they tried to find out which
Indian had stolen it, and then punished him.

MOTHER. — No; they at once set fire to the whole
town, and burned it to the ground; and then they
set fire to their fields of corn.

WILL. — But, mother, what was Raleigh doing?
I thought you said he was a good man.

MOTHER. — He was a good man, one who was
always kind to others. But he was not with the
settlers. Queen Elizabeth thought so much of him,
she could not spare him from England.

LIZZIE. — What did the Indians do, when they saw
their town burned down?

MOTHER. — They only went away to find another
place to live in. But they never forgot this cruelty.
They said to themselves, "We know now that these
pale-faced strangers are cruel. We cannot trust
them."

These first settlers did not stay long after this.
They went back to England. But they gave such

glowing accounts of the country — of its fine soil, its beautiful trees, and its rich fruits — that Queen Elizabeth was very much pleased. And she said, "This place shall be named Virginia, in honor of me." For Elizabeth was called the Virgin Queen.

LIZZIE. — I guess Raleigh was happy when he saw how pleased the queen was.

WILL. — If these people liked the country so well, why didn't they go back to it?

MOTHER. — Some of them did go back; and a great many others went with them. The most of these never left America again.

LIZZIE. — Why, mother, I thought you said the settlement was a failure. How could it be if some really staid in Virginia?

MOTHER. — This is the saddest part of my story to-night. About a hundred of the last settlers, men, women, and children, finding that their provisions were giving out, begged their governor to go back to England and get more supplies.

"I must not go and leave you," said the governor; "I must stay here to help you."

"But," said the settlers, "if you stay here, we shall all starve. It is better that you should go back for more provisions."

So the governor returned to England, leaving with the settlers his own daughter and her baby

4

girl,—the first white child born in America,—little Virginia Dare.

"We are glad the governor leaves his daughter and his little grandchild amongst us," they said; "we know he will come back quickly to help us."

WILL. — Well, didn't he?

MOTHER. — Yes; but he was delayed. And when the ships got back to America, not a single white person could be found. It was never known whether they went to live with the Indians, or whether they starved to death.

So, Lizzie, you see I was right in saying that many of the settlers did not return to England, and yet the Virginia settlement was a failure.

LIZZIE. — I see now. It was very sad.

WILL. — I should think Raleigh would have felt bad about it.

MOTHER. — He did; and it is said he sent out companies of men five different times, hoping they might find the missing ones. But the poor settlers were never heard of again.

WILL. — I thought you said Raleigh had more to do with colonizing America than any other man. I don't see that he really did much.

MOTHER. — He did not succeed in giving any lasting homes to the European people, it is true; but those whom he sent over brought back three things which had a great influence on both countries afterwards.

First, potatoes had never been seen in Europe till Raleigh caused them to be brought over. There had been terrible famines in Europe before this. But since people have found how easily potatoes can be raised, the poor have not suffered so much for want of food.

In the next place, Raleigh brought over tobacco from America.

WILL. — Why, did not people ever use tobacco till then?

MOTHER. — Never in Europe. The English learned the habit of smoking from the Indians, and at first it seemed quite a strange thing in England.

One day Raleigh was smoking. His servant came into the room, and as he had never seen any one smoke before, he was very much frightened. He thought his master was on fire. He rushed out of the room, seized a bucket of water, and running back, threw it over Sir Walter.

LIZZIE. — That is what you would want to do to Will, if you saw him smoking — isn't it, mother?"

MOTHER. — I hope there will never be any occasion to try it.

WILL. — What was the third thing you were going to speak of?

MOTHER. — This is not so easy to tell you about; and yet it was more important than either of the other two. We might say that the third thing Raleigh brought to England was "good news from America." For every time a ship returned, all the people on board would tell what a lovely country America was! how easy it was to raise corn! and what great tracts of land one could get to own just by sailing over there!

No poor man could own land in Europe. And to know that there were millions of acres of land in America which no one was using, made many want to go there. Before Raleigh's day it was a great affair to sail across the Atlantic. But Raleigh sent out so many ships, and they came back so quickly, that people said, "It is not such a difficult thing to go to America, after all. We will go and see the country; and if we do not like it, we can come back in a little while."

So we can see that Raleigh opened the way, and made it easy for other settlers to go to America.

WILL. — I don't see why none of those sent over by Raleigh had good luck.

MOTHER. — It was because there were no men among them fit to be leaders. We always find that any great enterprise will fail, if there be not one man engaged in it who can think and plan for the rest.

Can you tell me now what place in the United States will always remind you of Sir Walter Raleigh?

WILL. — I suppose you mean Raleigh, the capital of North Carolina.

MOTHER. — Yes; this city was named for Sir Walter Raleigh, and it is built on the very spot where those poor emigrants lived who were never heard of after their governor went back to England.

WILL. — You said a moment ago that the settlers landed in Virginia. Now you say they were at Raleigh in North Carolina.

MOTHER. — I see why you are puzzled. Virginia once included North and South Carolina, which were afterwards made into separate states.

LIZZIE. — But, mother, I want to know what became of Raleigh. Was Queen Elizabeth displeased because he could not make the people stay in America?

MOTHER. — The queen was very angry with him at one time, but not for that reason. He married a lady without asking Elizabeth if he might. This vexed her so much that she caused him to be put into prison. She pardoned him afterwards; but Sir Walter was never again a favorite at court. And during the reign of the next sovereign, James I., Raleigh was beheaded, after having been imprisoned in the Tower of London for thirteen years. When we were in London we saw the little cell in which Raleigh spent so many lonely years. And we were sorry that so good and brave a man — one who took so much interest in settling our country — should have had such a gloomy end.

VI.

A COLONY WITH A LEADER.

WILL. — Mother, I want to hear how the next settlement in America succeeded. Was it long after Raleigh gave up trying to colonize Virginia?

MOTHER. — It was about eighteen years before any more people tried to colonize. Do you remember why the first settlement was a failure?

WILL. — You said it was because there was no man fit to be a leader.

MOTHER. — Then if I tell you that the next settlement was a success, you will know it was because there was one man who could think and plan for the rest.

LIZZIE. — Now I guess we are going to hear something interesting!

WILL. — Because we are going to hear about a smart man.

MOTHER. — Yes; I am going to tell you about a brave man. His name was Captain John Smith.

WILL. — Captain! Was he a navigator, too?

MOTHER. — No; he was at one time a soldier in

Austria; and when he was promoted for good service and bravery, he became captain. He was born in England. His parents were intelligent and kind people. As soon as he was old enough to read, he was anxious to travel. His father died when he was only thirteen years old; and soon after, he started off to see the world.

I should like to tell you how he went on foot through the different countries of Europe, and what strange adventures he had; but there is so much to tell you about him in connection with our own country, that I must hurry on to that.

When Smith was about twenty-five years old, he got tired of travelling in Europe, and he thought he would go home to England. At that time there were a number of people who were thinking of going over to America. Smith happened to meet the man who was getting up the party. His name was Gosnold.

LIZZIE. — Gosnold! What a funny name!

MOTHER. — This Gosnold had been in America; and Smith was very much interested in hearing him tell what he had seen there. Of course Captain John Smith, who could not rest till he had seen the principal countries of Europe, felt he must go and see America, too.

Nearly a year was spent in getting ready for the

expedition. And in December, 1606, three ships set out from England for America.

Can you tell me, Lizzie, how long this was after Columbus made his first discoveries in America?

LIZZIE. — Let me see. Columbus made his first discovery in 1492. From 1492 to 1592 is one hundred years; and from 1592 to 1606 is fourteen years.

WILL. — So the first *real* settlement in America was made one hundred and fourteen years after it was discovered.

MOTHER. — You are right. And can you tell me who was King of England when Raleigh died?

WILL. — I guess I shall not forget that. It was James I. And I shall always be vexed whenever I hear any one speak of him; because he gave orders to have poor Raleigh's head cut off!

MOTHER. — While Captain Smith and others were fitting out their ships, Raleigh was in prison, awaiting his death. So now you know who was king during this next American settlement.

WILL. — James I.! Humph! Then I know things did not go just right with the settlers.

MOTHER. — If James I. had been a different kind of man, he might have made things much pleasanter for them. He said to himself, "Now these people who are going to America are all *my* subjects.

I must do something that shall make them feel my power, even when they are across the wide ocean." So he made plans for governing the settlers, and put the papers containing them into a box, which was not to be opened till they reached America. The names of the men who were to take charge of the new government were not even made known.

WILL. — Then I'm sure they got into trouble. For if any little quarrel came up, who was to settle it?

MOTHER. — You are quite right. There were hard times on the voyage over. Their minister, Rev. Mr. Hunt, a gentle, good man, tried to smooth matters, and then the quarrelsome ones turned upon him. Captain Smith tried to defend Mr. Hunt, by saying he was right and they were wrong. What did they do, then, but take Captain Smith and put him in chains! They kept him confined till they reached America. But when they found his name was in the box as one of those who were to govern, they let him go.

LIZZIE. — What did Smith do, mother, when he was free?

WILL. — I know what I would have done. 'I would have written to England and made a complaint.

MOTHER. — Then you would not have been such

a help to the colony as Smith was. He did not stop to think of his own wrongs at all, but went right to work to make the settlers comfortable.

LIZZIE. — Where did they land, mother? Just where the other poor settlers landed, who were never heard of again?

MOTHER. — They intended to land at the same place — Roanoke Island. Perhaps they thought they might find traces of their other countrymen. But a severe storm came on, so that the ships were driven as far north as Chesapeake Bay. The storm proved a blessing; for they had a much better place than the other settlers had had. Here they anchored, and a large party went on shore to explore. Soon they met five Indians, who were so frightened that they started to run. But the captain of one of the ships told the Indians by signs that they felt very kindly towards them. So they were not afraid any more, but invited the party to go and visit their little town.

WILL. — That is what I should like to see — an Indian town.

MOTHER. — The Indians treated the party as generously as they knew how to do. They gave them corn-cake, and tobacco and pipes; then entertained them with a dance. This meant that they were very glad indeed to see the white people.

After the party returned to their ships, they left Chesapeake Bay, sailing up a river which flows into its southern part.

Take your map, and see if you can find the river.

WILL. — I see it — James River. I suppose they called it after that mean king, James I.

MOTHER. — It was the month of May. The woods on either side of the river were full of singing birds. The air was fragrant with spring blossoms; and the hills were beautiful with fresh verdure. The little company of emigrants were enchanted.

After sailing up James River about forty miles, they came to a peninsula. This site was so lovely, commanding so fine a view of the river and sur- rounding country, that they chose the spot for their settlement. They named this place after their king, too. Look again on the map and find it.

LIZZIE. — I see it. You must mean Jamestown.

MOTHER. — Yes. After landing, the men whose names were in the box formed themselves into a government, and chose a president.

WILL. — I hope they chose Smith.

MOTHER. — On the contrary they left him out of their government altogether.

LIZZIE. — Did Smith want to go back to England then?

MOTHER. — No, indeed. He showed the same

manly spirit he did before, when they treated him so unfairly. He went right to work for the good of all, as if nothing had happened.

Of course the thing to be done now was to clear away the forests, and get materials for building. At first, it being a novelty, every man went to work with a good will. But soon many of the settlers got tired of this, like children who get tired of building block houses; so they left off working, and wondered if there was not an easier way to get along.

Smith, who had seen so much of the world, knew that the only way to have a successful settlement was through hard work. He did all he could to inspire the rest with courage and hope. He divided the work, and made plans for the little town they were commencing.

WILL. — Didn't Captain Smith go and get acquainted with the Indians?

MOTHER. — Yes, indeed. But he did not go far away from the settlers during the first summer. He was afraid they would leave off building. And if they did so, how could they live through the coming winter?

But cold weather came on, and Smith saw that there were houses enough for the settlement. The ships that brought them over had gone back to

England. Their provisions were nearly gone, and they did not know where to get more.

Lizzie. — Why didn't they go into the fields, and get corn and such things?

Mother. — They had no fields of corn. You must remember they had to clear away the forests before they could get a place even to build houses upon.

Will. — And that took so much time, they didn't have a chance to plant.

Mother. — That is so. And if it had not been for Smith, they would all have starved.

Will. — I think I know how he got something for them to eat! He went to the Indians.

Mother. — You have guessed right. Smith said to himself, "These Indians must have plenty to eat. They must have provisions laid up to last till spring. Perhaps I can get them to open a trade with our settlement, and thus obtain all we need." So, in company with several men, he started up a river that flows into the James, quite near Jamestown. See if you can find it.

Lizzie. — I see the name — Chickahominy.

Mother. — Smith went up the Chickahominy as far as he could in his barge. Then he left it, and went higher up the river in a canoe, with only two Englishmen, and two Indians who promised to show the way to their town.

After sailing about twenty miles, he left his canoe, with the men, and in company with one of his Indian guides, went on shore to shoot game.

Indian Canoe.

He had been gone but a little while, when two or three hundred Indians, with their cruel chief, surprised the men in the canoe.

"Shoot them! Kill them!" yelled out the chief. Upon that the Indians let their arrows fly till the two men were dead, stuck full of arrows.

LIZZIE. — O, how glad I am that Captain Smith had left the canoe!

MOTHER. — The Indians saw by the boot-tracks on the shore that there were more men in the company. So they started off in the direction Smith had gone.

Smith saw them coming, and knew by their horrid yells that they meant to kill him.

"If I appear frightened, it is all over with me," said he to himself.

So he bound his Indian guide to his arm for a shield, and looked carefully at his fire-arms, which he always carried loaded. As soon as the Indians came near, he fired off his gun so rapidly that he killed three Indians and wounded several others. The Indians had never heard a gun before, and they were so frightened they did not dare go near Smith. Keeping his eye on the Indians, he tried to make his way back to the canoe. But the first thing he knew he was up to his waist in a bog. Even then they did not dare come near him till he threw away his fire-arms.

WILL. — I don't see why he did that.

MOTHER. — Because he was almost dead with cold.

LIZZIE. — What did the Indians do then?

MOTHER. — They drew Smith out of the freezing mud, and carried him to a fire, and carefully rubbed his stiffened limbs. As soon as he could speak, he asked to see their chief.

Smith had in his pocket a very pretty ivory compass. He gave this to the chief, and showed him how the little needle always pointed to the north. The Indian was amazed.

Soon after this they marched him to a large Indian settlement. He was led by six great savages. When they got to the Indian town, they fed him so generously that he suspected they were going to fatten him and then eat him; for he knew that savages did sometimes eat people.

WILL. — I should think he would have been too much frightened to eat.

MOTHER.—Smith never lost his courage. After he had been with the Indians a few days, he found they were making great preparations to attack Jamestown. They came to him for advice and help.

John Smith and the Indians.

WILL.—Now I know why they did not kill him!

MOTHER.—He was glad enough that they had spared his life thus far, for he was again able to be of service to the settlers. He told the Indians that

5

it was a very dangerous thing for them to try to destroy Jamestown, that every man there had guns and swords, and that there was a great fort filled with loaded cannon. This frightened them so much that they gave up all thoughts of attacking Jamestown.

Soon after this they led Smith around to show him off to the different tribes near the three rivers which flow into Chesapeake Bay, north of the James. See if you can find these rivers on the map.

LIZZIE. — There is the James; and next comes York River.

WILL. — The river north of that is the Rappahannock, and the next is the Potomac.

MOTHER. — Very good. So, you see, Smith had a chance to become acquainted with the country.

WILL. — With the Indians, too. And that is what he wanted.

MOTHER. — The Indians were as curious to understand Smith as he was to know them. Did the Great Spirit send him to bless them, or was he the messenger of evil? One day he puzzled them very much. He took a piece of birch bark and wrote a message on it, and then sent it by some of the Indians to Jamestown. Could this white man make chips talk? What would he do next? Should they treat him as a friend or a foe. They danced around him to please him. They made hideous yells to frighten him. Finally, they led him before Powhatan, who was king of the tribes in that part of the country.

An Indian Village.

VII.

A NOBLE INDIAN GIRL.

MOTHER. — Powhatan was a tall, noble-looking savage. When Smith came before him, he was seated on a wooden throne. He wore a great robe of raccoon skins, and on his head a coronet of feathers. He was surrounded with attendants — Indian men and women, painted red, black, or white, and wearing strange-looking ornaments. Some of them had rings in their noses.

The whole crowd gave a shout when Smith entered. One, who seemed to be queen, came and washed his feet, and wiped them with feathers.

After they had feasted him generously, the Indians had a long talk with Powhatan, as to what should be done with him.

LIZZIE. — O, I hope they didn't kill him!

MOTHER. — Among the strange-looking groups, Smith saw a beautiful young Indian girl. From the number of attendants about her, he judged her to be a princess. This was Pocahontas, the king's daughter. She seemed to know what the Indians were talking about; for her dark eyes looked anxiously first at Smith and then at her father.

At last it was decided that Smith should be killed. Two large stones were placed before Powhatan. Smith was dragged to the spot, and his head was laid upon the stones. The great club of one of the cruel chiefs was raised, to beat out Smith's brains; when Pocahontas, leaping through the crowd, threw herself before Smith, and clasping his head in her arms, cried out, —

"Kill me! kill me! He shall not die!"

Powhatan's face showed at first surprise, then anger, then tenderness. The chief's great club fell to the ground.

"Let him live!" said Powhatan.

And so the little colony at Jamestown was again saved.

WILL. — That's what I call a noble girl!

LIZZIE. — Did Smith have a chance to talk with her after that?

MOTHER. — O, yes. He took a great deal of pleasure in making little things for Pocahontas to wear, such as strings of beads, bells, and copper ornaments.

Pocahontas had a brother, a fine, manly fellow, who also took a fancy to Smith, and did many kind things for him.

LIZZIE. — I am glad some one treated him well at last. It seems as if he had met with nothing but hard treatment ever since he left England.

MOTHER. — For several days Powhatan was undecided what he should do with Smith. Finally he tried to frighten him by having two hundred Indians howl around him in the most direful manner. Then he said, —

" We are now friends. Go back to Jamestown. Send me two guns and a grindstone, and I will give you much land, and love you as my own son."

Smith did not believe him. He expected every moment to be killed. But he reached Jamestown in safety at last.

The grindstone was too heavy to send back. But he gave the Indian guides a great many little presents for Powhatan and Pocahontas, which pleased them more than the grindstone would have done.

LIZZIE. — O, mother! didn't he see Pocahontas any more?

MOTHER. — Yes, indeed. Pocahontas was always a true friend to Smith. Not long after this, she found that the Indians were again intending to make an attack on Jamestown; and she hastened alone through the woods, on a dark and stormy night, to warn Smith of the danger.

WILL. — Then she saved the colony a second time.

MOTHER.— I think that is true. And I am quite sure she saved it at still another time.

During the winter, after Smith had been so long with the Indians, the poor settlers suffered much from hunger.

" I will carry them food," said Pocahontas. And every four or five days, all winter long, Pocahontas, with her attendants, walked over the snow and ice, carrying baskets of provisions to the starving people.

WILL.— I hope the settlers began to find that Smith was their best friend !

MOTHER. — I am sorry to say that they found fault with him because he did no more for them. They were very much vexed because he did not encourage them to give up planting and building, and search for gold.

At last they said, " We *will* dig for gold. We will send a vessel to England full of gold dust; and then our friends will see what we are doing."

When the ship which they loaded arrived in England, its cargo proved to be nothing but glittering dirt.

Soon after this, Smith had still harder times. More people came over from England. But they were not real workers. They were such people as England was glad to get rid of.

WILL. — That was enough to discourage any man.

MOTHER. — Smith kept on working for the colony; trying to rouse the idle, and have each one work for the public good.

After a while the wives and daughters of many of the settlers came out to them.

LIZZIE. — Perhaps that made the men go to work; for they would be ashamed not to have decent homes for their families.

MOTHER. — They did much better after this. The houses began to look home-like, and soon they built a little church. But in the mean time Smith met with an accident. Some gunpowder exploded, and injured him so much that he was obliged to go back to England, — there being no surgeons in America who could dress his wounds properly.

LIZZIE. — O, mother! was that the only pay he got?

MOTHER. — If we look at it in one way, we might say it was; for he did not own a foot of land in America, — not even the house which he had built with his own hands. But Smith's conscience told him he had done the best he could. And the world has ever since thanked him for doing what he did for America. He was, in fact, the first man who succeeded in establishing a colony in this country.

Columbus discovered America. The Cabots discovered that portion of America best fitted for colonization, and claimed it for England. Sir Walter Raleigh gave to the world the desire to colonize America. But Captain John Smith, by hard labor and much self-sacrifice, *first established homes in America.*

LIZZIE. — I guess Pocahontas was sorry to have Smith go away!

MOTHER. — She must have been very sorry.

After Smith left the colony, she had much to do with its history. A party of the settlers went back into the country to forage — that is, to pick up food, or anything else that would be of use to them. After stealing everything they could lay hands to, they saw Pocahontas coming; and they said, "Let us carry her off! We will make the old king buy her back." So they carried off Pocahontas, and sent word to Powhatan that he could not have his daughter unless he would pay a large sum for her.

WILL. — To think of treating Pocahontas like that, after all she had done for the colony!

MOTHER. — Powhatan was enraged at the insult; and he said, "I will never buy her back! I will fight for her!" And many of the Indians became enemies to the English.

But just at that time a young Englishman, named John Rolfe, took a great fancy to Pocahontas. And Pocahontas liked him very much. So they were married. Powhatan was pleased at this; and he never allowed any of his tribe to be unkind to the English afterwards.

LIZZIE. — Did Pocahontas live in a wigwam after she was married, or did she live in a house like ours?

MOTHER. — She did not live in a wigwam any longer. And when she was twenty-one, she went to England with her husband, and saw the king and queen.

Indian Wigwam.

Everybody showed her a great deal of attention. I think Smith had something to do with this. For when he heard Pocahontas was coming to England, he wrote a letter to the queen, telling her how much good Pocahontas had done to the colonists, and begging the queen to be very kind to her. He also said that it would make the Indians in America feel kindly towards the English, if they should hear that Powhatan's daughter had been treated like a princess.

But true, brave, noble, devoted Pocahontas remained as simple as when she roved in the forests around her father's hut.

WILL. — I don't believe she forgot Smith, either.

MOTHER. — She had heard that he was dead; when one day he was suddenly presented to her!

Now, you know people at court must be very ceremonious — that is, they must bow just so, and speak to each other in just such a way, or they are called rude.

When Pocahontas saw Smith, she forgot all about court manners ; and, rushing across the room, she flung her arms around him, and called him "father!"

She felt hurt when Smith told her that such freedom might do for the wild forests of America, but not for the English court. She turned away from him, hid her face in her hands, and did not speak for two hours.

Then she said, " You were not afraid to come to my father's country, and cause fear in him and all his people but me! And fear you *here* that I should call you father? I tell you, then, I *will!* And you shall call me child! And so I will be forever and ever your countryman!"

WILL. — I should almost know Pocahontas would talk like that.

LIZZIE. — Did she like living in England?

MOTHER. — I think she could not have enjoyed giving up her native freedom. And then the climate did not agree with her.

Her husband was just going back to America with her, when she died, leaving a beautiful little boy. This little boy staid in England till he had received a good education; then he went to Virginia, and became a rich man. It is said that some of the first families in Virginia are descended from him.

LIZZIE. — Since you told us about Columbus, I have thought he could not have discovered America if it hadn't been for Isabella. Smith could not have colonized America if it hadn't been for Pocahontas.

MOTHER. — I think we may safely say that. Pocahontas was just the friend Smith needed. Isabella herself could not have been to Smith what Pocahontas was.

WILL. — And Pocahontas could not have helped Columbus as Isabella did; because she was not rich.

MOTHER. — You are quite right. And we may learn from this that God gives to earnest souls just the help they need to carry out his plans.

WILL. — Did Smith ever go back to America?

MOTHER. — It seems as if the settling of America was what he loved and cared for more than anything else in the world, for he had no family. And as soon as his health was better, he was again busy in his chosen work.

He did not go back to Jamestown, although the settlement there did not prosper for a number of years after he left it. But he explored the land in what we call New England. He made maps of it, and also of the country between New England and Virginia. He wrote books, describing the climate, soil, and appearance of the country. He told of the advantages there were in going to a large country where each one could have land of his own, and grow rich if he was willing to work. And people were more anxious than ever to go to America.

Smith did not live to be an old man. He died in London in the year 1631.

WILL. — That was twenty-six years after he went to Jamestown. So he must have been fifty-two years old.

MOTHER. — I am glad to see you remember our talks so well.

What colony was first settled, Lizzie, and who was the father of it?

LIZZIE. — Virginia was the first, and Smith settled it. If the settlement was not a very happy one, it was because there were so many men in it who didn't like to work.

MOTHER.— I had almost forgotten to tell you another bad result of the idleness of the first settlers.

In 1619, a Dutch ship arrived at Jamestown, landing twenty negroes. "Here!" said the Dutchmen to the Virginia planters; " you are in want of workers. Buy these slaves, and you will have no trouble in raising corn and tobacco."

The negroes were bought and set to work, with the fear of the whip-lash on their backs if they dared to be idle. In this way slavery was brought to this country.

LIZZIE. — Couldn't the poor negroes have any land of their own?

MOTHER. — No; they were bought and sold with the land.

LIZZIE. — That wasn't right. So I am sure the Virginia colony would have to suffer for it some time.

VIII.

THE HOME OF FREEDOM.

MOTHER. — Before saying much about the settlement at Plymouth, I must go back and tell you why these people wanted to come to America.

WILL. — You said the first settlement in America did not succeed because there was no man fit to be a leader. Are you not going to tell us about some smart man among those who went to Plymouth?

MOTHER. — I am going to tell you something about a great man, though he was not one of the settlers.

You know, when we were talking about Columbus, we said that God let him believe that the world was round, and made him feel sure that there was another continent, because all Europe needed to know it.

LIZZIE. — Yes; the merchants wanted to find an easier road to India.

WILL. — The Portuguese navigator got the start, though, and found the way to India by doubling the Cape of Good Hope.

MOTHER. — All Europe would soon after need to know that there were homes to be found in America, and for a reason a thousand times more important than that for finding a passage to India.

You must know that the governments in Europe were very strict. That is, they gave the people very little freedom, — especially the poor people.

WILL. — I remember you said a poor man there could not own any land.

MOTHER. — The discovery of America made a great change all over the world. It was wonderful news to learn that there was a great country across the ocean. It was like opening a window in a dark and crowded room, so that sunshine and fresh air could come in. Everybody was thinking and talking about it; and thinking and talking make men's minds grow. It was just before this time, too, that printing was first used.

LIZZIE. — Why, mother! didn't people have books to read before then?

MOTHER. — They had only books that were written by hand. These were costly; and of course but very few could afford to own them. The common people could not have read them either, if they had owned them. But now they were beginning to read and to think for themselves.

I told you just now that the European governments did not give the people much freedom. One proof of this is, that men were not allowed to worship God each in his own way. Every man had to pay something out of his small earnings to support the same kind of church, and say, I believe so and so. And if he did not do this, he was punished by law.

WILL. — I don't think that was fair!

MOTHER. — When people began to think for themselves, they saw it was not fair. But it was a very dangerous thing for a man to say so.

About this time there was a very bold, brave man in Germany, named Martin Luther, who dared to say, "Every man must think for himself. No man can think for him!"

Martin Luther was like a lion among men. He would say what he believed, even if he knew it would cost him his life to say it.

LIZZIE. — Was Martin Luther among the Plymouth settlers?

MOTHER. — O, no, dear child. He died before the first settlement at Jamestown. The reason I am telling you about him is, that he had something to do with the coming of the settlers to Plymouth.

Martin Luther loved music. He wrote beautiful hymns for the people to sing. These grand old hymns, that were first sung in Germany, echoed

6

from country to country, till all Europe was quivering with their music. People *sang* about freedom before they dared to talk about it. Thus music was a mighty weapon against the tyranny of kings.

LIZZIE. — I like to hear you talk about it, mother, because your voice is so deep, and you look so earnest; but I cannot quite understand you.

WILL. — I do. Mother means that the people were all singing of freedom before the kings knew what they were about.

MOTHER. — Thank you, Will. You are right. Sitting here by the pleasant fire, and hearing only our own low voices, it is an easy thing to say, "Every man must worship God in his own way." But this thought from Heaven made every king in Europe tremble on his throne. It was the cause of the most horrible wars.

Europe was not large enough for this mighty thought to grow in. People began to say, "We cannot think, — we cannot breathe freely here. We must have more room."

WILL. — Now I see the whole of it! Of course the kings were not willing that the people should think as they pleased; and so folks said, "If we can't think about God as we want to here, we will go where we can. We will go to America!"

MOTHER. — That is it. So, you see, the time had

come when it was really necessary that the people of Europe should know of a place like America.

WILL. — Then the discovery of this country did more good than just finding a passage to India would have done.

MOTHER. — Far more. Columbus little knew what great good was coming to the world through the mighty feeling in his heart which impelled him to his discoveries.

LIZZIE. — I can see why people should have liked to go to America: it was a new place, and people like to see new places.

But do you think the settlers who came to Plymouth would have been treated very badly if they had staid in Europe?

MOTHER. — I cannot begin to tell you how cruelly people were treated who dared to believe in God in their own way. They were hunted like wild beasts. Many were banished from their country forever. Many were burned to death. In France alone, one hundred thousand people were put to death for believing what they thought was right.

WILL. — A hundred thousand! How could it be?

MOTHER. — There was a cruel king in France at that time. His mother was a very wicked woman. And then there was a duke who was also very cruel. These three, who had most to do with the government, thought no more of killing men and women than you would of killing flies. And they said, " What business has any one to think differently from kings and queens ! We will show people what they ought to believe ! "

So they had a party, and invited thousands of people to come to it. It was a great affair, for it was to celebrate the marriage of a prince. And just as everybody was having a good time, the word was given, " Kill ! Kill ! "

This was the beginning of one of the most terrible times the world ever knew. A hundred thousand men, women, and children were put to death.

And all this was for believing in God as they thought right.

WILL. — O, how angry the people must have been all over Europe !

MOTHER. — And instead of believing just what the kings said they must, there were larger numbers than before who said, " We *will* think for ourselves ! "

This horrible affair in France occurred over a hundred years before people began to come to America to live. But after this a great many persons in England were burned to death for worshipping God in their own way. And the Plymouth settlers, who could not meet together to talk about

God without being disturbed, did not know but they would be hunted down or driven from their country.

They said, " We would rather live in huts in America, and have quiet talks about God, than stay here."

So you see the hundred men, women, and children who left England in the ship Mayflower did not come to America to make discoveries, or to hunt for gold. They came to worship God in freedom.

LIZZIE. — O, it must have been hard for the little children who were with them! Was it very cold weather when they started?

MOTHER. — They left England in September, 1620.

WILL. — That was fourteen years after Captain John Smith left for Virginia.

MOTHER. — When the Pilgrims first left their homes the weather was pleasant and warm. The gardens were full of flowers; the hills were green; the birds were singing.

After the Mayflower had been tossing on the stormy ocean for sixty-three days, the Pilgrims were told they had reached their new homes. The little company crowded on deck, full of hope; for they had heard pleasant things of America.

O, how bare and bleak everything looked! No green fields, no blossoming meadows. The hills were covered with snow. The leafless branches of the trees were encased in ice, through which the winter winds moaned. The rocky coast, as far as the eye could see, was white with frost. Even the sunshine remained behind the clouds, as if to make the picture colorless and bare.

LIZZIE. — O, mother! Didn't they all want to go back to England?

MOTHER. — No. "This shall be the home of Freedom!" they said. "Here we can worship God." And they joined in singing a hymn — one of the hymns that Martin Luther had taught the people.

WILL. — I don't believe these folks had any quarrelling on the way over.

MOTHER. — They did not. And before they went on shore they signed a paper, saying each would work for the good of all. They also chose one of their number for a governor, — one whom they all loved, and were willing to obey. His name was John Carver.

When they lowered their little boat to go on shore, they found that it needed repairs. It had served as a sleeping berth on the voyage over. They had to wait seventeen days before it was fit to use. In the mean time sixteen of the men put themselves under the command of Captain Standish, and reached the shore by wading through the icy water. This gave them severe colds, from which some of them never recovered.

WILL. — I don't see why they needed a captain.

MOTHER. — They had heard of the Indians. And in case of attack, they knew they must have one man to look to for orders.

WILL. — That shows they were more sensible than the men at Jamestown, who were always quarrelling because every one wanted to be captain.

MOTHER. — When the little boat was ready, a number of the men again started to hunt up and down the coast for a good harbor. It was snowing fast. The spray from the waves froze upon them, so that they had on coats of ice.

After exploring the coast in different directions, they landed and made a fire, staying on shore through the night. The next morning, just at daybreak, they heard the horrid yell of the Indians. And soon the air about them was full of arrows. But no one was hurt. Thankful for this, they started off again, in their little shallop, to search for a good harbor for the Mayflower.

As the day wore on the storm increased. The snow and sleet so blinded them that it was difficult to get a glimpse of the land. Their little boat rose and fell like a feather on the foaming waves. Soon

Pilgrims seeking a Harbor in the
Storm.

their rudder broke. Then their mast was split in pieces, and the sail went overboard. Night came on. "We are lost!" cried they; and each thought of the dear ones in the Mayflower, who were anxiously waiting for them.

But just then they found themselves in a little bay, where they were sheltered from the fury of the storm. The war-whoops of the Indians were still heard in the distance.

"Let us thank God for his care!" said the Pilgrims. "He has saved us from the dangers of the storm; He will guard us from the savages." And so He did.

Numb with cold, and almost perishing with hunger, they landed and built a fire.

By the light of the next morning they saw that they were on an island at the entrance of a good harbor, where the Mayflower could be safely moored.

LIZZIE. — How singular! When the Jamestown settlers were trying to land, a storm drove them into a good deal better place than they expected to find.

WILL. — It drove them into Chesapeake Bay, near James River.

MOTHER. — And the storm which the Pilgrims met drove them into what we now call Plymouth Harbor.

Overcome by cold and fatigue, they were glad to rest during the next day, which was Sunday. On Monday morning they again started to explore the harbor, and find the best landing-place.

They soon came to a large rock by the shore, which seemed to invite them to stop. Here they moored their little boat.

And on the 22d of December, 1620, these stout-hearted, earnest men stood upon the shores of Plymouth, and thanked God for Freedom.

LIZZIE. — And they were glad they had found a good place to make homes for the mothers and the little children — were they not, mother?

MOTHER. — Indeed they were. They explored the country a little, and found that the forests were partly cleared away. They found beautiful springs of water. They also found a heap of corn.

" We will go back now to the Mayflower," they said, " and tell our friends we have found a good place for a settlement."

What do you think had happened while they were gone? A dear little baby boy had been born. He was named Peregrine White. This was the first English child born in New England; and he lived to be over eighty years old.

WILL. — It must have been a good deal easier to make a settlement here, than if no forests had been cleared away.

MOTHER. — That is true; although they had many hard times during the winter that followed, and were in constant fear that the Indians would drive them away.

LIZZIE. — I don't see how they kept the little children warm till they got houses built.

MOTHER. — Fortunately the Mayflower did not go back to England till April. So the women and children had comfortable quarters on board till the huts were ready for them. But the climate was very hard upon all the little company. They had never felt such severe cold in England. And when spring came, half their number had died. Among these was their good governor, John Carver.

LIZZIE. — O, what a hard time they must have had! I pity them more than I did the other settlers, because there were so many mothers and little children. They were such good people, too! I wish they had gone farther south; then they would not have suffered so with the cold.

MOTHER. — They intended to go a little farther south. They meant to land at the mouth of Hudson River.

WILL. — I suppose they had learned about the place from Smith's maps.

MOTHER. — They had learned, too, that some Dutch settlers had already landed there, and liked the place much. But they were never sorry that they chose Plymouth for their landing-place.

WILL. — I want to know if they went and got acquainted with the Indians, as Smith did.

MOTHER. — After they had been at Plymouth about six months, an Indian one day walked boldly into town, saying, " Welcome, English! Welcome, English!"

LIZZIE. — That is strange! I thought the Indians could not speak our language.

MOTHER. — This one had learned a little English from some fisherman on the coast of Maine. The settlers received him very kindly. They learned from him that many Indians had formerly lived at Plymouth, but a terrible pestilence had swept them from the land. They also learned that Massasoit, the king of all the tribes in the neighborhood, was near by, and that he wanted to open friendly relations with the settlers.

In a few days they were again surprised by a visit from Massasoit himself, accompanied by sixty of his followers.

WILL. — Sixty Indians! Why, there were not so many settlers as that!

MOTHER. — It was an anxious time for the little band of Pilgrims. Massasoit did not come at once into town, but was stationed on a hill within sight. The governor sent word that he should be glad to talk with the Indian king. He also sent him some presents, — two knives, a copper chain with a jewel in it, some "strong water" or whiskey, a quantity of biscuit, and some butter. This kindness assured Massasoit that the settlers would do him no harm. So, accompanied by a few followers who had laid aside their bows and arrows, he approached the little town. The settlers received him with as much pomp and ceremony as it was in their power to do. Captain Standish, with six musketeers, went out to meet him.

Massasoit allowed himself to be conducted to an unfinished house, in which were placed a green rug and three or four cushions. Soon the governor advanced, attended by a few soldiers, two of whom made a great flourish with a drum and trumpet. Refreshments were then served; after which a treaty was agreed upon, in which Massasoit promised to be a good friend to the English, and to help them in case they were attacked. In return the governor promised friendliness on the part of the English.

This treaty was of great use to the English in many ways. It was kept sacred for over fifty years.

LIZZIE. — Then I am sure there were some good-hearted Indians.

MOTHER. — The colony gradually increased in numbers. In a year from the time they landed another party of emigrants came over from England. But this was a great drawback to the success of the colony during the next winter.

LIZZIE. — Why, I should think they would have been glad to see more English people!

MOTHER. — So they were, at first. But these last settlers had no provisions; and the first comers had to share all their food with them. Such was their trust in God they did not complain, but gave cheerfully to the strangers.

WILL. — Couldn't they get corn from those Indians who were so kind to them?

MOTHER. — No; these Indians were very poor, and, like themselves, did not know one day where they would get anything to eat the next.

LIZZIE. — Why! Were the Pilgrims so poor as that?

MOTHER. — At one time they had so little corn that each family could have but a single pint. When this was parched and given around, they could allow but five kernels at a time to each person. After this they had no corn at all. And for months you would have seen nothing on the best table among them but a lobster, or a bit of fish, and a pitcher of water.

It was four years before they had any cattle; so, during all that time, they had but little meat. They did not go without bread, however, after the second winter.

LIZZIE. — If they had no cows or goats, then the little boys and girls could have no milk!

MOTHER. — I had not thought of that.

WILL. — And, of course, they could get no butter nor cheese.

LIZZIE. — I guess they were glad when summer came, for then they could get berries.

WILL. — They could shoot birds, too, and catch fish in the streams.

Did they have good luck in planting? If they had no cattle, it must have been hard work to get the ground ready.

MOTHER. — They did not have all the corn they needed during the first two years. Instead of each man's planting for himself, all worked in common. That is, they worked together, and then divided the corn equally.

WILL. — I don't think I should have liked that. If I were willing to work more hours than another man, I should feel as if I ought to have more corn.

MOTHER. — So some of the Pilgrims thought after working in this way for two years.

As soon as each man had his own little plot of ground to plant, everybody became interested to see how much corn he could raise. The consequence was, that they not only raised enough for themselves, but they had some to sell to the Indians, and to the fishermen who came near the coast.

WILL. — I don't see why the Indians wanted to buy. I should think they could have raised corn of their own.

MOTHER. — So they could. But the Indian loves

to rove and hunt better than to cultivate the ground. And if he can buy corn with the furs he gets in the chase he is glad.

WILL. — The settlers must have felt encouraged, if they could raise corn enough to buy furs with. If they got more furs than they needed, they could send them over to Europe and get money for them.

LIZZIE. — But how could they send them, when there were no ships going back?

MOTHER. — Soon after this there were more ships going and coming across the Atlantic. Though the settlers suffered so much, they kept up good courage, and wrote back such pleasant accounts to their English friends, that more people came over. "We are happy," they wrote. "We have given up many home comforts that we had in England; but we can worship God in our own way. What more can we ask?"

IX.

ALONE IN THE WOODS.

MOTHER. — In 1629, — nine years after the May-flower came over, — one hundred people arrived, and made another settlement at Salem. And one year later, fifteen hundred settlers came. Many of them were highly educated. Before they started they chose John Winthrop for their governor. He was a very kind, unselfish man. He loved Old England ; yet he felt indignant that kings should meddle with what he thought about God.

Among the people who came over with him were some who had lived in such rich homes, that they would have been discouraged at the prospect of living in the miserable little houses of the new country, if it had not been for his cheering words.

LIZZIE. — Did all these people go and live with the Plymouth settlers ?

MOTHER. — No; they landed first at Salem. After-wards some of them settled at Boston, some at Charlestown, and some at other places along Massa-

7

chusetts Bay; so that they were called the Massachusetts Bay Colony.

LIZZIE. — The Plymouth settlers must have been glad to know there were so many more people from England in the country. They could go and see them sometimes.

WILL. — And trade with them, as they did with the Indians.

MOTHER. — It was really so. Then, too, each colony chose a few men and sent them to Boston, to talk over what was for the best good of all.

This was the beginning of civil government in America. The whole were governed by a few men, and these men were chosen by the people themselves.

WILL. — The Pilgrims must have liked that better than to be governed by a king they hadn't chosen, and perhaps didn't like. Besides, a king stays a king as long as he lives; and if he is a bad man, the people can't help themselves. But if a governor doesn't do the right thing, why, the people can choose a better man.

LIZZIE. — A governor would let people think as they liked.

WILL. — Of course. The people wouldn't choose a man who would not do that.

MOTHER. — Well, now I am going to tell you something that will surprise you very much.

LIZZIE. — What is it?

MOTHER. — The first dispute the Pilgrims had was about letting every man think as he liked about serving God.

WILL. — Why, they came over to this country, because they wanted every man to do that!

MOTHER. — Certainly they did. I will tell you how the trouble began.

A little while after the company had settled in Salem, a very good young man came over from England and landed at that place. His name was Roger Williams. He was only thirty years old; but he was a fine scholar and a true gentleman. By that I mean he was always making others happy, wherever he went. This Roger Williams was a minister; and he left England because he was not allowed to preach what he thought was right.

LIZZIE. — Then I should think the Pilgrims would have liked him.

MOTHER. — So they did, until they found that he did not believe just as they did. You see, by this time, a great many people were coming over from England. Some liked to go to church, and were willing to pay to help support it; while others did not care to go, and were not willing to pay any money for it.

WILL. — I suppose they wanted their money for other things.

MOTHER. — No doubt. They were already start-ing schools, and perhaps some felt more interested in them. But, at any rate, the laws of Massachu-setts said, "Every man must go to church. Every man must give something to support the church."

WILL. — Then if the laws said so, the men that made the laws must have all believed alike about it.

MOTHER. — The few men who came over from Europe at first did all think alike. But you can see that when people came over by thousands, there must have been many who did not think as the Pil-grims did.

When Roger Williams saw that they punished people for not going to church, he said, " Your laws are wrong ! It is right to punish a man for stealing, but not for staying away from church."

The Pilgrims did not see it so ; and they said, " You must not teach our children such wicked notions as these. Men who will not go to church are not fit to take part in the government. We want no such men here. But Roger Williams was firm. He said, " I left my native land because I could not speak the truth as I saw it. You may banish me from the country ; you may take my life ; but you shall not take away my freedom !" Yet all this time he was so kind-hearted, that those who lived near him loved him. They even chose him for minister at Salem. But when the people at Boston heard of it, they were very indignant; and they sent word to Salem that Roger Williams was a very unsafe man for a preacher. "He is trying to overthrow our government," they said.

To this Roger Williams replied, "I am not trying to overthrow your government; I am trying to prevent you from doing that yourselves. Your laws are not wise, if they do not provide for the good of all. I believe that God has chosen this great country to be an asylum for the poor and oppressed of all lands. And how can that place be home to a man where he cannot enjoy his religion?"

WILL. — Did the Pilgrims agree with him then?

MOTHER. — No; and the people of Boston, where the courts were held, were so indignant at the Salem people for making Roger Williams their minister, that they took away a large tract of land belonging to them. They also declared that the Salem settlement should no longer be under their protection.

This made the Salem people sorry for what they had done. So they wrote a letter to the governor at Boston, and said so.

WILL. — Then the Salem people were cowards.

MOTHER. — At last Roger Williams had no friend

left who believed in him. Even his wife, Mary, thought he was wrong.

" If I cannot stay here and believe and say what I think is right, I will go to another part of the country," said Roger Williams.

But the people at Boston heard of this, and determined to send him out of the country altogether.

WILL. — He must have been a smart man, if they were as afraid of him as that !

MOTHER. — He was ; and too wise a man to be caught. For when the officers went into his house to arrest him and put him on board a ship that was just ready to sail for England, he was gone, no one knew where.

LIZZIE. — Did his wife go with him ?

MOTHER. — No ; and it was fortunate she did not ; for during the next three and a half months he was wandering through the snowy forests, often without food, and with no shelter but a hollow tree.

LIZZIE. — O, that was too bad !

WILL. — I didn't think the Pilgrims could treat a man so — an honest man, too ! Why, I think he was the truest, best man of them all. Of course he was not going to help them make a government like the one they had left in England.

MOTHER. — No, indeed ! And his heart was so

Roger Williams searching for a Sleep-
ing-place in the Wilderness.

large that he thought not only of the good of those already in America, but he thought of the millions that might come from all lands in the future. But if Roger Williams was homeless, he was not without friends.

WILL. — Then I know who would be kind to him, — the Indians!

MOTHER. — You are right. He found a welcome in every Indian hut which he entered. He was no stranger to the red men. He had often visited their lowly homes, and had learned something of their language. After a while he came to Massasoit's humble dwelling; and the kind-hearted king, who had before promised friendliness to the English, now gladly opened his door·to the homeless man, and showed him a generous hospitality.

At another time Roger Williams visited some Indians farther south, called the Narragansetts; and their chief, Canonicus, usually thought to be a very cruel Indian, loved him as his own son.

WILL. — Did Roger Williams stay long among the Indians?

MOTHER. — Not long. He was anxious to start a little colony somewhere out of Massachusetts, and have a government which would not meddle with the churches at all. Just then he received a letter from Governor Winthrop, which surprised him very much.

LIZZIE. — Who was Governor Winthrop?

WILL. — Why, I remember; he was governor of Massachusetts.

MOTHER. — You are right. His letter gave Roger Williams the unexpected hint to go to Narragansett Bay and settle, as no Englishman had as yet any claim to the land.

Roger Williams took this advice. By that time five old friends had joined him, saying they wanted to help him make a new settlement. So, in June of 1636, — sixteen years after the Pilgrims first landed at Plymouth, — Roger Williams and his five friends got into a canoe, and paddled down a little stream that flows into Narragansett Bay. They stopped at the head of the bay, at a place that seemed to be a pleasant spot for a settlement.

"The providence of God has cared for me, and led me hither; therefore I will name the place Providence," said he. And it has been called Providence ever since.

LIZZIE. — Why, that is the capital of Rhode Island!

MOTHER. — And now you know who founded Rhode Island. This land belonged then to the Narragansett Indians. But when their chief, Canonicus, found that his white friend, whom he loved so dearly, was going to settle there, he made him a present of a large tract.

LIZZIE. — What could he do with so much land?

MOTHER. — Roger Williams had been there but a little while, when many others joined him from the different settlements. And some came from England to Rhode Island, having heard that the most freedom could be found there.

Roger Williams gave his land away freely to those who were not able to buy it for themselves.

So that he had only as much left for himself as the humblest stranger among them.

LIZZIE. — Did he always live in Rhode Island after that?

MOTHER. — Always. But he visited England in a few years, to get a charter for the colony.

LIZZIE. — What do you mean by a charter?

MOTHER. — It was a paper from the King of England, saying that his people in America might govern themselves and choose their own officers. The Massachusetts colony had such a charter; and Roger Williams was glad to receive one for Rhode Island, too.

Nothing better shows us what a good man he was, than the fact that he always loved and spoke well of the Massachusetts Bay colony, even after they had driven him from his home into the wilderness.

He lived to be seventy-seven years old; and died as he had lived, beloved of many.

X.

MORE COLONIES.

MOTHER. — Tell me the names of the colonies you have already heard about.

LIZZIE. — Virginia, Massachusetts, and Rhode Island.

WILL. — Didn't you tell us that some Dutch people went to New York?

MOTHER. — Yes. When it was found that the English had not discovered the north-west passage to India, the government of the Netherlands — or Holland and Belgium — said, "Perhaps we can find it. We ought to, if any one can; for we own more ships than all the rest of Europe."

So they fitted out a large ship, and gave the command of it to Henry Hudson.

LIZZIE. — Now I know where the Hudson River got its name.

MOTHER. — I see you are guessing out my story. Six years before the Puritans landed in Massachusetts, Hudson sailed up the beautiful river which is called after him; and he was disappointed when his vessel could go no farther.

WILL. — He knew then that *he* hadn't found the way to India.

MOTHER. — Yes; and this was such a disappointment to Holland, that he was not sent again. But a great many Dutch people came to America after this, and settled in what we now call New York and New Jersey.

LIZZIE. — That makes two more settlements. So we now know of five colonies.

MOTHER. — The Dutch did not come over for the same reason that the Puritans did. They were mostly traders. They bought furs of the natives, and sent them back to Europe. They put up the Dutch flag at first, thus showing that they claimed the country for Holland. But afterwards some of their governors did not treat them well; so they were glad to pull down the Dutch flag, and live under the English flag.

Have you noticed that all the people who came over to America settled along the coast?

WILL. — Of course. They could not get far into the country on account of the forests.

MOTHER. — You are right. If you will look at your maps, and follow along the coast, it will be easy for you to tell me the names of the Thirteen Colonies that were first settled. Begin at New Hampshire.

WILL. — New Hampshire, Massachusetts, Rhode Island, Connecticut, New York, New Jersey, Pennsylvania, Delaware, Maryland, Virginia, North Carolina, South Carolina, Georgia, —

MOTHER. — There, you have named thirteen.

LIZZIE. — Did all the other settlers suffer as much as those you have told us about?

Settlers Emigrating to Connecticut.

MOTHER. — No; but nearly all suffered from the cruelty of the Indians. The later the settlement, the less trouble did they have.

The Connecticut settlers had a hard time. About

fifteen years after the Puritans landed, a large colony of men, women and children emigrated from Massachusetts to Connecticut. They started in the fall of the year, driving their cattle before them. Their only guide was a compass. Their bed at night was the rocky hill-side. If it had not been for the milk of the cattle, many little children would have died; for their march through the wilderness was so much more difficult than they had expected, that they did not reach Connecticut till after winter had set in, and their provisions had given out.

LIZZIE. — What made them go to Connecticut?

MOTHER. — They had heard it was a beautiful place, and that the land was made rich by a large river and its branches.

WILL. — That was the Connecticut River.

MOTHER. — In the following year a large company from England joined them. After this they had less suffering.

There was one other New England colony of which I must tell you. New Hampshire was settled in 1623 by a few English merchants, who built little houses along the principal rivers. The settlement did not increase so rapidly as the others.

If you will look again at your maps, beginning at New Hampshire, you will find I have told you something about every colony till we reach Delaware.

Delaware was settled by a company from Sweden. They had very little trouble with the Indians, for they were protected by the surrounding colonies. As the settlement increased in size, the Dutch in New York became jealous, for they felt they had the first claim to the land. So they drove the Swedes away.

WILL. — But you said that the Dutch lived under the English flag after they had been in this country a few years.

MOTHER. — This was after Delaware was taken from the Swedes. So you see the little colony was claimed at different times by three nations, — first by Sweden, then by Holland, and finally by England.

As there is nothing else very striking in its story, we will pass on to Maryland, — the colony that was settled with the fewest hardships. It is a beautiful spot; and the Virginians were very anxious to include it within their colony. But twenty-seven years after Jamestown was settled, a company of Catholics sailed up the Potomac. They had been sent out by Lord Baltimore, to whom the English king had given a grant of land.

LIZZIE. — Why did they have an easy time?

MOTHER. — They arrived in the spring of the year. Lord Baltimore, who was very wealthy, had provided generously for their comfort. Their leader, Calvert, was a good and wise man, who made only such laws as were for the good of all.

WILL. — Then he didn't punish people for not thinking all alike — did he?

MOTHER. — No. And this was the principal reason why the Maryland settlers were happy: each man was left in freedom to think for himself.

LIZZIE. — Of course they would agree, if they were all Catholics.

MOTHER. — But other people, who did not agree with them in religion, went afterwards to Maryland, and were left in perfect freedom.

WILL. — You said just now that these Catholics came over twenty-seven years after John Smith did. Then they must have landed in 1633; and that was three years before Roger Williams went to Rhode Island.

MOTHER. — Can you think of a city that was named after the man who sent out the Maryland settlers?

LIZZIE. — I can, — Baltimore.

MOTHER. — North and South Carolina were settled by people from England, Holland, and France. Many from the northern colonies joined them.

WILL. — You haven't told us anything before about folks coming over from France; but I should think they would have been glad to come, for you said that a hundred thousand people were killed there at one time.

MOTHER. — You are right. There were many in France who thought as the Puritans did. They were called Huguenots. About fifty years after the Puritans landed, a great many Huguenots went to what we now call North and South Carolina. The first settlers were very glad to have these Frenchmen come, for there were many fine workmen among them, — mechanics, and artists. The other countries in Europe would gladly have welcomed them; for their industry and taste for the fine arts enriched every place they settled in.

WILL. — Did the French king give them a charter?

MOTHER. — No; they had been so persecuted at home, that they lost all love for the French government; and they were glad to live under the English flag. There was no American flag then, you know.

I am sorry to say that the Huguenots suffered much during their first year or two in America. But it was well that they went to the Carolinas, for the climate there is much more like sunny France than in the other colonies.

8

XI.

A FRIEND TO THE INDIANS.

WILL. — Can't you tell us about some other brave man that had strange adventures?

MOTHER. — You know there are two colonies of which I have given you no account yet. I hope the story of the one I am to tell you about now will interest you. It was started by a man who believed he could get along peaceably with the Indians; and he always did. His name was Penn; and the colony was named after him.

WILL. — Penn! Then you are going to tell us about Pennsylvania!

MOTHER. — Which means "Penn's Woods." William Penn was born in London. He was a Quaker, — that is, he was one of those who believe it is wrong to go to war, or even to defend one's self in danger, save by kindness and love. He also believed that all men are equal in the sight of God, — that rich and poor, high and low, educated and ignorant, share alike the Heavenly Father's love. "Why, then," said he, "should one do homage to a king, more than to any other man?" "No," said he and the other Quakers, " we will not take off our hats even in the presence of nobles or kings."

This got the Quakers into trouble, — particularly William Penn, whose father was an admiral in the English navy, and who often attended the king's court. Of course the son was known at court also.

LIZZIE. — Was William Penn's father a Quaker?

MOTHER. — He was not; and he was so vexed to find his son would carry his Quaker manners into court, that he drove him from home. He might never again have noticed William, if the kind mother had not pleaded for him. But she urged the father so much to take pity on the wanderer, who had no money and no place to lay his head, that finally the father forgave him.

WILL. — I should think the court people, too, would have been vexed at Penn, if they knew why he kept on his hat.

MOTHER. — They were very angry with him. After a while he was looked upon as such an enemy to the government, that he was arrested and put into prison. But this did not alter his love for the Quaker faith. He afterwards travelled in Holland and Germany, preaching with such earnestness that many people who heard him became Quakers.

WILL. — Then they must have had to suffer, as the Puritans did.

MOTHER. — Yes.

LIZZIE. — I think I know what would happen next: the Quakers who had to suffer would want to go to America.

MOTHER. — That was so. William Penn did everything in his power to help the Quakers. He wrote books to show that the governments had no right to trouble them if they did no real wrong. He also freely said this whenever he met any of the king's friends.

WILL. — I shouldn't think he would have met the court people after he had been arrested.

MOTHER. — His pleasant manners and kind, generous heart always made him a favorite at court in spite of his views. At one time, even the king took great notice of him.

LIZZIE. — Perhaps William Penn thought it was a good plan to make friends at court, so that he could help the Quakers.

MOTHER. — I think that was his chief reason in so doing, for his own tastes were very plain and simple. But when he found there could be no peace for the Quakers in Europe, he was very anxious to be the means of providing comfortable homes for them in America.

When Penn's father died, the king was owing him a large sum of money for important military services.

WILL. — Then the king ought to have given the money to William Penn.

MOTHER. — Yes, he ought. But Charles II. was a very extravagant king, and never had any money to spare. So when Penn offered to take, instead of the money, a tract of land in America, Charles II. gladly consented. And in August, 1682, William Penn and a number of Quaker friends sailed for the Delaware. reaching that river after a voyage of six weeks.

WILL. — In 1682; that was seventy-six years after the Jamestown settlement.

LIZZIE. — And sixty-two years after the Puritans came to Plymouth. So he must have had a good deal easier time than they did.

MOTHER. — Yes. There were already a number of Quakers near the Delaware; and when Penn landed, they flocked about him and gave him a hearty welcome.

A few days after this, Penn took a boat, and with a few friends sailed up the river till they came to a peninsula formed by the meeting of two rivers — the Delaware and Schuylkill. Mooring their boat, they scrambled up the river-bank. It was a sunny

day in October.   As they stood under the elm trees
on the high spot of ground which separated the two
streams, and looked over the country, beautiful with
autumn foliage, William Penn said, "I have seen
the finest cities of Europe, but I never saw so beautiful a site for a city as this!"

WILL. — Then didn't he choose that place to settle in?

MOTHER. — The land was already claimed by some
people who had come from Sweden.   But Penn was
so charmed with the situation that he bought the
land from the Swedes, and it soon became the principal place of the settlement.

William Penn took great interest in laying out
and beautifying it.   He said he hoped the place
would always be noted for the kind feeling of its
people.   So he called it Philadelphia, which means
" brotherly love."

WILL. — You said that Penn had no trouble with
the Indians.   Were there many about there?

MOTHER. — There were nineteen tribes in and
around Pennsylvania.   Of course William Penn had
never known any Indians till he came to America.
But he reasoned thus about them: " Is not God the
Father of the red man as He is of us?   And should
we not love *all* his children?"

So William Penn went among the natives with

the feeling that he was no better than they; and he always treated them with loving courtesy.

A few weeks after he landed, he sent word to the various tribes around, that he would meet them on a certain day to make a treaty. At the time set, crowds of the tawny-skinned natives assembled under the elm trees a little way north of Philadelphia.

William Penn was then thirty-eight years old, graceful and fine-looking; and as he stood before them in simple dress, surrounded only by a few Quaker friends, every Indian heart was moved to love him as he uttered these words:—

"I will not call you children, for parents sometimes chide their children too severely; nor brothers only, for brothers differ. The friendship between you and me I will not compare to a chain, for that the rains might rust or the falling tree might break. We are the same as if one man's body were to be divided into two parts; we are all one flesh and blood."

LIZZIE.— The Indians must have liked that. What did they say?

MOTHER. —They said: "We will live in love and peace with William Penn and his children, as long as the sun and moon shall endure." This treaty never was broken.

Lizzie. — And that was because he really loved the Indians.

Mother. — During the year following the treaty, William Penn often met the Indians at their councils or at their festivals. He visited them in their cabins and shared their roasted corn and hominy. He laughed and frolicked with the little pappooses, or joined in the out-door games of the warriors. Some-

Penn accepting the Hospitality of the Indians.

times he talked with them about religion. He found that they had faith in God, whom they called the **Great Spirit**. They believed the Great Spirit made all things, and that he loved his children. No

Indian was afraid to die, because they fully believed that better hunting-grounds were awaiting them, if they had been good Indians, — had been brave, hospitable to strangers, and had never broken a promise.

LIZZIE. — With so many good friends around them, I don't see why the Pennsylvania settlers could not have had an easy time.

MOTHER. — As long as William Penn staid among them, everything went along pleasantly. People from other countries in Europe who were looking to America heard that great freedom of thought was allowed to every man in Pennsylvania; and also that there was no trouble with the Indians. For these reasons the settlement grew more rapidly than any of the others.

In 1683, Philadelphia consisted of three or four little cottages. In two years after, there were six hundred, also schools and a printing-press: so that in three years Philadelphia had grown more than New York city had done in half a century.

WILL. — Then William Penn did not always remain in America.

MOTHER. — No; he went back to England to help the Quakers, many of whom were imprisoned. He afterwards returned to this country, remaining only two years however, when important business called him again to England.

After this came the most severe trials of his life. His son, whom he had sent to Pennsylvania in his stead, not only neglected his affairs, but disgraced him by habits of dissipation. Another trouble also came: a man with whom he had intrusted his money matters in America, proved dishonest, and got Penn in debt to a large amount, so that he had to go to prison.

LIZZIE. — O, dear! it seems as if the good men always had to suffer.

MOTHER. — This was hard on Penn, for he was then sixty-four years old. After remaining in prison for many years, he was set free by the help of friends. He did not live long after this, and died at the age of seventy-eight.

Although terrible times frequently arose between the different colonies and the natives, it is said that no Quaker blood was ever shed by an Indian, — so much did the red man love and honor the name of William Penn.

I am sorry to say that in after years the descendants of this good man did not show the same loving, unselfish spirit which he had done in managing the colony.

You have now heard something about twelve different colonies.

WILL. — Georgia is the only one you have not told us about.

MOTHER. — There is nothing very interesting to tell about it. It was the last colony established, having been settled one hundred and twenty-seven years after the first settlement of Jamestown.

WILL. — That must have been in 1733.

MOTHER. — You are right. Now please look on the map and tell me again the names of the thirteen colonies.

XII.

THE PEQUOD WAR.

WILL. — You said, in our last talk, that some of the colonists had trouble with the Indians. Please tell us about it.

MOTHER. — In order to do so, we shall have to go back to the time when Connecticut was first settled.

WILL. — That was when the company of emigrants left Massachusetts for Connecticut, about fifteen years after Plymouth was settled.

LIZZIE. — Which made it about 1635.

MOTHER. — That is right. As soon as they had finished their weary march through the wilderness, before they had completed their miserable little huts, they had constant attacks from the Indians.

LIZZIE. — It wasn't the tribe that was so kind to Roger Williams — was it?

WILL. — You mean the Narragansetts.

MOTHER. — It was a much larger tribe than the Narragansetts, and far more fierce and cruel. They were called the Pequods, and numbered seven hundred warriors; while the colony could only muster two hundred soldiers.

LIZZIE. — What made the Indians so cruel to the whites?

MOTHER. — They felt that Connecticut belonged to them alone, and that the English had no right there.

The Pequods had been deadly enemies of the Narragansetts for a long time. But when they foresaw that the English were likely to get all the land into their hands, they went to Canonicus, the chief of the Narragansetts, to see if he would join them against the English, and kill or drive every white man from the country.

This was a perilous time to the Connecticut settlers. "If the two **tribes** unite against us," said they, " we must give up at once. If we could only get Canonicus to join with us, we should be safe."

WILL. — The settlers must have known how much Canonicus thought of Roger Williams. Why didn't they get him to go and say a good word for them?

MOTHER. — That is exactly what they did do. And Roger Williams showed the generosity of his heart when, starting off alone in a poor canoe, he hastened through a driving storm to the home of Canonicus, to plead for those who had once driven him into the wilderness.

The bloodthirsty chiefs of the Pequods were already there. For three days and three nights, Roger

Williams ate and slept with them, knowing that at
any moment his throat might be cut. Finally, through
his gentle influence, the Narragansetts decided to
remain friendly to the English.

Indians attacking the Settlers.

But the Connecticut
settlers were never for a
moment safe. Wherever
they might be, in the
field, around the fire-
place, or singing songs of worship in their little
churches, they were liable to be attacked by the
cruel Pequods. At last, the settlers could endure
it no longer. They must protect the homes of their

wives and children. And in the year 1637 began the terrible Pequod war.

The English, headed by Captain John Mason, and aided by the Narragansetts and a few other tribes, made an attack on the principal fort of the Pequods. It was just before dawn. The Indians were sleeping. While the English soldiers were ascending the hill on top of which stood the fort, a watch-dog barked an alarm. The Indians awoke and hastened to the fight. They numbered nearly three times as many as the English, and it seemed as if they must conquer.

"We must burn them!" shouted Mason; and he threw firebrands among the light mats of the wigwams. In a few moments, the whole encampment was in a blaze. Six hundred Indians — men, women, and children — perished in the flames; while only two of the English had fallen in battle.

In a few days, more troops came from Massachusetts. The other Indian villages were attacked; every wigwam was laid in ruins. Their chief fled, and was afterwards killed by a hostile Indian. Of the few Pequods remaining, some joined the Narragansetts; the rest were sold by the English into slavery. Thus perished the tribe of the Pequods, and the Connecticut settlers rejoiced in victory.

LIZZIE. — But, O, mother, how they must have

felt when they thought of the Indian mothers and little children that had been burned to death!

WILL. — Yes; but their own mothers and children would have been killed, perhaps, if the Pequods hadn't been destroyed.

LIZZIE. — I don't believe it! They might have offered to buy the land. They might have treated the Indians as William Penn did afterwards; then they wouldn't have had to be so cruel.

MOTHER. — There is no doubt that the Pequods were more fierce and cruel than the tribes in Pennsylvania; but I feel sure that more kindness on the part of the white people would have brought about a different treatment from the Indians.

XIII.

KING PHILIP'S WAR.

WILL. — What other colony had quarrels with the Indians?

MOTHER. — The Massachusetts and Plymouth settlements, — or we will say the Massachusetts colony, as the two were united.

LIZZIE. — Why, I thought the treaty with the great Indian chief —

WILL. — Massasoit —

LIZZIE. — Yes; — I thought the treaty with Massasoit wasn't broken for over fifty years.

MOTHER. — You are quite right. And it was not till after his death that the troubles began. Massasoit always showed a very kind feeling toward the whites. During the Indian war of 1637, he used his influence to keep the different New England tribes from uniting with the Pequods against the English; and it is said that this Indian chief and Roger Williams had more to do than any one else in saving the New England settlements from destruction by the natives.

9

Massasoit frequently did things to show friendliness to the English. At one time he sent his two sons to the court at Plymouth to receive new names.

"My sons shall be no more called by the name of their fathers," he said. "Let them receive new names, that you may know I love you and yours, and desire to have you feel kindly to me and mine."

So the two sons gave up their Indian names, and were called Alexander and Philip. The oldest, Alexander, became king of the Pokanokets when Massasoit died. He always showed the same kind feeling toward the whites that his father had done.

WILL. — Then I don't see how any trouble could come.

MOTHER. — As the settlers in Connecticut had suffered such losses at the hands of the Indians, they were always watchful and suspicious lest the tribes in their neighborhood should turn against them. At one time they heard that Alexander was their enemy, and that he had asked the Narragansetts to join with him in a war against the whites.

WILL. — I don't believe that of a son of Massasoit.

MOTHER. — Without waiting to see if it were true or not, Alexander was in a haughty manner ordered to appear before the Plymouth court.

LIZZIE. — Had they any right to order him to go, mother?

MOTHER. — Alexander thought not, and refused to go. Upon this, Captain Winslow with a force of ten men was sent to arrest him. They surprised Alexander and his followers, not many miles from his home at Mount Hope. Then they took away the arms of the little Indian troop, and Captain Winslow, pointing a pistol at Alexander, said, " If you stir, or if you refuse to go back with us, you are a dead man ! "

Alexander was at first so astonished that he could not speak. Had he deserved such treatment? Was this the return for the kindness shown them by his father during the last fifty years? It was too much to bear. A raging fever crept into the veins of the proud king. A sudden weakness seized him, and in faltering accents he asked if he might go home. He was allowed to go ; but he *died upon the way.*

WILL. — Well ! if the Indians didn't rise and have a fight after that, then I'm mistaken. I should like to know how the Massachusetts people would feel, if their governor were treated so. I tell you what ! I wouldn't blame the Pokanokets if they had driven every white man out of the country.

MOTHER. — Upon the death of Alexander, Philip became king of the Pokanokets. The thought of his brother's death was like a thorn rankling in his heart. It is true that he appeared at the Plymouth and Boston courts, and promised kindness to the whites. For several years, it seemed that he meant to carry out the kindly intentions of his father. But every year the English wanted more and more land; so that the hunting-grounds were continually becoming smaller, and they had fewer fishing-streams to depend on.

LIZZIE. — That must have been hard for the poor Indians, when they had once had the whole land to roam over.

MOTHER. — Philip foresaw that if nothing were done to stop the whites, the time would come when his people would be driven from their birthplace. Should he be a coward, and die a slave; or should he rouse his people to fight for the land of their fathers? The settlers wanted them to swear that they would be faithful to the king of England. What did they care for a far-off king they had never seen? If the English king let his people behave as the settlers had done, they did not want to have anything to do with him. Besides, the whites tried to force a religion upon them which they did not like. They enjoyed their own religion best, which they felt was given them by the Great Spirit.

All these grievances made Philip resolve to get the tribes throughout New England to fight for their country and their rights.

An affair soon occurred which hurried Philip into war before he was fully prepared. An Indian by the name of Sassamon had been educated by the settlers, so that he might become a teacher among his own people. He had even been through college.

LIZZIE. — Why! did they have schools and colleges then?

MOTHER. — Certainly. The New England settlers started common schools in a very few years after they came over. Harvard College was founded in 1636; and it was here that Sassamon got his education. After this he was private secretary to Philip; that is, he did all his writing.

WILL. — Then he must have known all about Philip's affairs.

MOTHER. — Exactly: and that is how the trouble commenced. Sassamon suddenly left him, went to the governments at Plymouth and Boston, and told them all about Philip's plans.

WILL. — The traitor!

MOTHER. — Soon after this, Sassamon was murdered, — by whom, no one knew. But three Indians were arrested by the settlers, declared guilty, and put to death. One of these Indians was a particular friend of Philip's.

WILL. — That made him angry again.

MOTHER. — He at once ordered his tribe to send

all their women and children to the Narragansetts for safety. And soon the cry of " War ! war ! " went through the New England colonies. This was in June, 1675.

Philip is said to have wept when he first heard that English blood had been shed by some of his tribe.

LIZZIE.—I suppose that was because his father's treaty was broken.

MOTHER. — The colonists declared that the war against Philip was just.

WILL. — Of course.

LIZZIE. — O, dear ! war is dreadful ! I wish they had not treated the Indians so, after Massasoit died.

Did Philip's people have to suffer as much as the Pequods did ?

MOTHER. — The stories are somewhat alike ; but I think King Philip's war was the sadder of the two, because the Pokanokets had been such good friends to the English, helping them in many ways.

WILL. — Yes ; and the Pequods always hated the Connecticut settlers.

MOTHER. — Remembering what the Connecticut people had suffered, the Massachusetts colonists were filled with horror. They at once raised troops to fight the Pokanokets. In a week after the war commenced, Philip was driven from his home at

Mount Hope; and he flew from one tribe to another, to engage them to fight on his side. Soon, town after town was attacked, the houses plundered, and many of them set on fire. There was no rest for the settlers, day or night. If the farmer went out to feed his cattle, there was no certainty he would ever come back. Even the mother with her little babes was not safe, and she fled in terror from one town to another.

WILL. — I should think the soldiers might have been on the lookout, so as to keep off the Indians.

MOTHER. — The Indians have a different kind of warfare from the English. Instead of going in a large body in open day, they would lurk behind trees, or hide in muddy swamps which no white man dared to enter. Then they would steal out and surprise the whites.

WILL. — What did the Narragansetts do? Did they join Philip?

MOTHER. — At first they promised to join the English. But after Philip had been fighting several months, driven about from one place to another, and having lost a large number of his warriors, he was nearly destitute. In this condition he went to the Narragansetts for safety and help. Canonchet, their present chief, received him with open arms.

WILL. — That didn't suit the English.

MOTHER. — No; and they determined to strike a blow that should ruin both chiefs at once, and put an end to the war. A large body of soldiers was raised in all the colonies, and sent into the Narragansett country. It was mid-winter, and the swamps being frozen and leafless, the Indians could not escape the English so readily as in summer. Canonchet, fearful of an attack, had sent the greater part of his stores, together with the old, the sick, the women and children of his tribe, to a kind of Island in the middle of a swamp. Here Philip and himself had gathered their warriors, and had carefully built a kind of fortress, which hid the wigwams.

LIZZIE. — You said Philip had sent his women and children to the Narragansetts; so I suppose some of them were in the fort too.

MOTHER. — Yes; and the two chiefs thought they had built the fortress so strong that nothing could happen to the dear ones within. But the English, guided by a native who had turned traitor to Philip, plunged through the snowdrifts and took the Indians by surprise. Then came a fierce and cruel fight. At first the English were driven back, and several of their bravest officers were killed; but soon they gained ground. The Indians, driven from one post of the fortress to another, fought with the fury of despair. Most of their warriors were cut to pieces; and after a long and bloody battle, Philip and Canonchet retreated from the fort, and fled to a forest near by.

LIZZIE. — And what became of the Indian mothers and little children?

MOTHER. — The English set fire to the forts and to all of the wigwams; and most of the old men, women, and children perished in the flames.

LIZZIE. — O, mother! I should think Philip and Canonchet would wish they had died too.

MOTHER. — When they saw the flames, and heard the cries of their helpless ones, they filled the woods with yells of rage and despair.

WILL. — And did the settlers believe all this was right?

MOTHER. — They were sorry the wigwams were burned, for, being far from home, they had no roof to shelter them from the winter storms.

LIZZIE. — How could they stop to think of themselves, when all the poor Indians were suffering so!

MOTHER. — It is said that when the colonists saw the terrible suffering they had caused, they felt troubled, and some asked themselves if this was the way God would have the Indians treated.

LIZZIE. — You said *most* of the women and children were killed. What became of the rest?

MOTHER.—They hid themselves in a cedar swamp, with nothing but evergreen boughs to shelter them from the cold. They pawed up the snow to gather nuts and acorns, till they sank down from weakness and hunger. Thus perished the tribe of the Narragansetts.

LIZZIE.—Poor Indians!

WILL.—But what became of Canonchet?

MOTHER.—He would not give up, even after his terrible losses. "We will fight to the last man," he said, "rather than become slaves of the English!"

Being pursued by the colonists, he was finally taken prisoner; and when told that he was condemned to die, he said, "I like it well! I shall die before my heart is soft, or before I say anything unworthy of myself!"

WILL.—And what became of Philip?

MOTHER.—He was discouraged and almost broken-hearted by the death of Canonchet, for they had loved each other tenderly. But he was not quite desolate, for his wife and little son had never left him. After the defeat of the Narragansetts, he wanted to look once more upon his native land. So, with his loved ones and a few warriors, he visited Mount Hope. But O, how changed was the home of his boyhood! Only ruin and desolation everywhere.

But even here there was no rest for him; for the settlers did not feel safe so long as they knew that the king of the Pokanokets was living. Early one

King Philip visiting his Ruined Home.

morning he was surprised by the English, most of his warriors were slain, and his wife and son were made prisoners. The broken-hearted chief, with a few followers, fled to a swamp where the muddy pools were hidden from sight by low shrubs.

LIZZIE. — O, they wouldn't hunt down a poor

Indian when he was so badly off! Philip couldn't do any harm now.

MOTHER. — As they were cut off from all the necessaries of life, one of his followers said to Philip, "It is no use to fight any more. Why not give up to the English?" "Give up? Never!" said Philip; and he shot the coward warrior dead at his feet.

A brother of the Indian that was killed was so provoked at this, that he ran over to the English and told where Philip was. A party of the settlers soon surrounded the swamp. Philip fought till every follower was slain; then, turning to fly, he was shot dead.

LIZZIE. — And his wife and little boy?

MOTHER. — I don't know what became of Philip's wife after she was taken prisoner; but Philip's only son — the little prince who was to have become king of the Pokanokets — was sold into slavery.

WILL. — That was a handsome return for what Massasoit did for the settlers. I tell you what I think: the settlers didn't really believe the Indians were *men* like themselves. Anyhow, they acted as if they thought white folks were a great deal better than the red men. Now if they had only believed as William Penn did, — that they were men, and not wild beasts, — they would not have treated them so.

LIZZIE. — No; for they would have thought that God wanted all his children to be kind to each other.

MOTHER. — The settlers suffered greatly through the war. For fifteen months they had been exposed to constant attacks from the Indians, during which time they lost six hundred men. Thirteen towns had been burned to the ground, and eleven partly so. They also got largely in debt from the expenses of the war.

LIZZIE. — And the Pokanokets and Narragansetts lost everything.

WILL. — Think they did! There were no such tribes after this.

MOTHER. — True; the end of King Philip's war, in 1670, was the last that was heard of the Pokanokets or Narragansetts.

XIV.

KING GEORGE'S WAR.

WILL. — Were there any other such terrible times between the settlers and the Indians?

MOTHER. — Nearly all the colonies suffered more or less from the cruelties of the native tribes.

LIZZIE. — Pennsylvania did not.

MOTHER. — No; not while William Penn lived. The colonies were engaged in another war soon after King Philip's death; but this time the trouble did not begin in America.

Whenever England went to war against any nation in Europe, it was felt in this country.

WILL. — That was because there were people from those nations in the colonies — wasn't it?

MOTHER. — Yes. At one time, England had a war with Spain. Can you tell me which colonies would feel it most?

LIZZIE. — I think it must have been the colonies nearest the Gulf of Mexico, because the land which Spain owned in America was there.

MOTHER. — You are right. After this war was

over, England had several quarrels with France. The one I shall tell you about first was in 1744.

LIZZIE. — That was a long time after the colonies were settled.

WILL. — Not so very long after the settling of the southern colonies.

MOTHER. — Do you remember what France owned in America?

LIZZIE. — I do: Canada.

WILL. — I suppose the French went over and settled Canada, as the English did Virginia and the other colonies.

MOTHER. — Yes; and some of the French settlements were made before the English ones. Acadia, for instance, now called Nova Scotia, was settled before Jamestown.

LIZZIE. — They must have had dreadful winters, going so far north.

MOTHER. — It is not so cold as you might suppose it to be. It is a very beautiful spot. I shall have a story to tell you about Acadia, so do not forget where it is.

You have learned by this time that people in coming to a new country generally settle along the rivers.

WILL. — Of course. The land is better; and they can easily sail up the rivers from the ocean.

MOTHER. — So you can tell where the French probably settled in Canada, if you will examine your maps a moment.

LIZZIE. — I think, along the St. Lawrence: that is the largest river.

WILL. — And after a while they might follow up the river till they came to the great lakes, and start towns there.

MOTHER. — They did so. They had also formed settlements at Newfoundland.

The English had never disputed the right of the French to Canada; but now that England and France were at war, matters were very different.

WILL. — I suppose the French people in Canada thought they must fight the English in the colonies; didn't they?

MOTHER. — Exactly so. And England encouraged her colonies to take up arms against the French. She had little difficulty in doing this; for the colonies still dearly loved their mother-country; and her wrongs were their wrongs.

LIZZIE. — It seems hard that the settlers should have troubles just because the English and French kings had a quarrel. They had been through such dreadful times in making their homes in the first place, and then in fighting the Indians, I should think they would have been discouraged at the thought of more fighting.

MOTHER. — They were often disheartened.

WILL. — How was it with the Indians? Did they side with the French or English?

MOTHER. — Part of the Indians sided with the English, and part with the French.

WILL. — Then they had Indian wars again.

MOTHER. — Which made the times far worse for the colonists.

At one time a large number of troops was raised in New England, to make an attack on the strongest fort of the French. It was called Louisburg, and was situated on the Island of Cape Breton, at the entrance of the Gulf of St. Lawrence.

WILL. — I saw a fort once: there were cannons looking out of every window.

MOTHER. — There were a great many cannons at Louisburg. Take your maps and find it.

WILL. — I see it. I suppose when the English tried to sail past it, so as to get up the St. Lawrence, the cannons in the fort would fire away at them.

MOTHER. — Yes; and as the principal French settlements were on that river, the English thought they could not do better than to get possession of this great Gate of Canada, as it was called.

WILL. — I can see. Did they get it?

MOTHER. — Yes; but at the end of the war, when

10

the English and French kings were deciding what each should have, it was agreed that the fortress of Louisburg should be given back to France. This was very provoking to the New Englanders, after they had taken so much trouble and lost so many men in taking the fort for their king, George II.

Capture of Louisburg.

WILL. — I hope they let George II. do his own fighting after that.

MOTHER. — This war, called King George's war, lasted four years. After this the colonists had a few years of quiet.

XV.

HOW A POOR BOY BECAME A FAMOUS MAN.

MOTHER. — Just so surely as the needed rain and sunshine come to gladden the growing trees in spring-time, so surely did the men appear who seemed to have been born and fitted to help America in her times of greatest danger. One of these men was Benjamin Franklin, born in Boston in the year 1706. In his early childhood he might have been seen running about the streets — a little ragged fellow, as unconcerned as if making mud pies and sailing toy boats by the sea-shore were all he was born for.

WILL. — Didn't he go to school?

MOTHER. — Only for a little while. His father was poor, and was obliged to take him into his shop, to work at candle-making, when he was only ten years old. This business was very distasteful to Benjamin; but his father kindly gave him some time for play.

One of his favorite amusements was, in company with his mates, to fish for minnows in a creek not far from home; and the mother complained bitterly of the muddy boots and trousers that came home at night.

One day little Ben said, "Boys, this mud is a nuisance; and I know how we can get rid of it."

"How? how?" said the boys.

"Don't you see that big pile of stones the workmen have heaped up in that next lot? Come to-night after dark, and we will bring the stones all over here and make us a wharf."

"Hurrah! We'll do it! we'll do it!" said the boys.

So when night came, the boys went to work like so many little ants, tugging away, sometimes two at one stone. The wharf was finished.

The next morning, when the workmen came to commence their cellar, they were surprised and very angry at what had been done. They found out the names of the boys, and went and complained to their parents.

LIZZIE. — Franklin was most to blame.

MOTHER. — At first he could not see that he was to blame at all. "The wharf is very useful," he said.

LIZZIE. — Yes; but he stole the stones to make it of.

MOTHER. — After a while, Franklin's father convinced him that "*that which is not honest cannot be truly useful.*"

WILL. — If Franklin was to become very useful to his country, I don't believe he staid very long in his father's shop making candles.

MOTHER. — When he was twelve years old, his brother James opened a printing office; and the father gladly apprenticed Benjamin to his brother, for he knew Benjamin would like this business better.

LIZZIE. — Yes; for he would have a chance to see a good many books.

MOTHER. — When Franklin was fifteen years old, his brother James began publishing a newspaper. After a while, Benjamin wrote several articles for the paper himself.

" Now, if I let James know who wrote them," he said, " he will not think them worth noticing. I will disguise my handwriting, and put them under the door after dark."

When James found the pieces, he showed them to his friends; and Franklin heard them all wonder who could be their author. And when they decided it must be such a one, naming a man of great learning, he was very much encouraged. He went on writing for the paper, and did not tell his secret for a long time. But when he did, James was more envious than glad.

After a while, some of Benjamin's writings got his brother into trouble. Even at that age Franklin was much interested in the public meetings; and if anything happened which he thought unjust to the public, he at once spoke of it in the paper. Some of his pieces were aimed at what he thought was wrong in the government officers. And finally the colonial assembly felt themselves so much insulted, that James was arrested and sent to prison for a month; and he could not publish the paper after this.

The paper was continued for a while in Benjamin's name; but the whole affair caused James to treat his brother with unkindness, and even cruelty, so much so that Benjamin ran away to New York. Not finding employment there, he went to Philadelphia. Imagine how funny he must have looked when he arrived there. Here is his own account: —

"I was in my working-dress, my best clothes being to come by sea. I was covered with dirt; my pockets were filled with shirts and stockings. Fatigued with walking, rowing, and having passed the night without sleep, I was extremely hungry, and all my money consisted of a Dutch dollar and about a shilling's worth of coppers, which I gave the boatmen for my passage."

He went into a baker's shop and asked for a threepenny loaf. "The baker gave me," says Franklin, "three large rolls. I was surprised at receiving so much. I took them, however, and having no room in my pockets, I walked on with a roll under each arm, eating the third. In this manner I went through

Franklin's first Appearance in Philadelphia.

Market Street to Fourth Street, and passed the house of Mr. Read, the father of my future wife. She was standing at the door, observed me, and thought with reason that I made a very singular and grotesque appearance."

Lizzie. — Poor fellow!

Will. — Such a boy as that wasn't long without work, I know.

Mother. — He soon found employment in a printing-office, and happened to board with the father of the young lady who had laughed at his awkward looks.

Franklin first came into public notice when he was about twenty-one. The colony of New Jersey was about to issue paper money; and the printing of the bills came to Franklin's employer. The work had to be done in New Jersey, so that it might be carefully overlooked by the government officers. They soon found out that it was Franklin who invented ornamental designs for the bills, and who contrived the copper-plate press. "Look here!" said they; "this young fellow knows more about printing than his master! He is more kind and obliging too. He will get the business all into his own hands before long."

And this proved true. He was soon in business for himself, and became printer for the Pennsylvania colony, at the same time publishing a newspaper in which he freely gave his opinions about public matters. The paper was so much more attractive than any that had before appeared in the colonies, that it soon had a long list of subscribers.

WILL. — How Franklin did succeed in every-thing!

LIZZIE. — I suppose that was because he did everything so well.

MOTHER. — Most likely every one would succeed if he were as upright, industrious, prudent, and saving as Franklin was.

As he got older and saw that many failed in their undertakings while he succeeded, he was anxious that others should try his plan. To let people know the secret of his success, he published an almanac called "Poor Richard's Almanac." Every number contained wise sayings which people could easily remember, and which would lead them to be pru-dent and kind. He published the almanac annually for twenty-five years; and at the end of that time he collected all the proverbs into one book, which he called "The Way to Wealth." The wise sayings in this book were so much thought of, that they were copied into the newspapers of all the colonies, and were afterwards reprinted in England and France.

By the time Franklin was thirty he had got his business into such a prosperous condition that he could afford to give a large share of his time to the public good. First, he thought of his own city. To wake people up to improve their minds, he started a club. This club lasted for forty years, and then became the " American Philosophical Society," of which Franklin was first president. Franklin also influenced the people of Philadelphia to have the city paved and lighted; to have an orderly fire department; to have a public library; and to start good schools and colleges. So much can one man do, if he has the will.

WILL. — I should think he would have been a good man for governor, or something like that.

MOTHER. — He did hold many different offices in the course of his life, as you will see. The first was that of clerk to the Colonial Assembly. Afterwards he became postmaster. Whenever any public improvement was thought of, he was one of the first to be consulted. " If we can get Franklin to push it, it will go," people said.

LIZZIE. — But I suppose he wouldn't help unless he thought it would be a good thing for the people.

MOTHER. — No, indeed ! And that was why every one had so much confidence in him. They knew he had *common sense*. One of his mottoes was, " A man's truest good can be found in doing all the good he can to others."

With all the public and private business he had on his hands, he still found time for self-improvement. He learned the French, Spanish, and Italian languages, and afterwards the Latin.

After he had started many improvements in Philadelphia, he thought of the colony at large. As many members of the government were Quakers, nothing had been done to train soldiers; while Pennsylvania was liable to be attacked by foreign invaders as well as by Indians.

LIZZIE. — I thought you said William Penn made all the Indians about there behave well.

MOTHER. — So he did; but that was seventy years before; and many people had come to Pennsylvania who did not understand dealing with the natives. And through the influence of the French, the tribes on the borders of Pennsylvania began to take advantage of the whites.

WILL. — Did Franklin raise the soldiers?

MOTHER. — He went to work with his usual spirit, to show people the need. Then he roused them to enlist. It was not long before a large body of soldiers were ready in case of attack; and a fort was built on the river below the city.

WILL. — What did the Quakers say to that?

MOTHER. — Though he did not get much help from them, he found they were very willing that other people should defend the colony. His energy and common sense in this affair called forth the praise and thanks of the governor and council; and after this they consulted him whenever any important matter came up that concerned the colony.

It was about this time that Franklin made his great discoveries in electricity.

WILL. — I remember a story about that. Franklin had thought for a good while that lightning was the same as electricity; and one day he sent up a kite, pointed with wire, into a thunder-cloud, — and down came the lightning right into the ground.

MOTHER. — That was the way he came to invent lightning-rods, which have saved so many houses from destruction. This and other discoveries made him famous all over the world; and many colleges of Europe gave him learned titles on account of it.

LIZZIE. — And only think! he never went to school after he was ten years old.

MOTHER. — The next public service of Franklin was a benefit to the whole country. The post-offices had been a great expense to the government; and yet they were so poorly arranged that news travelled very slowly. Franklin was made postmaster-general of all the colonies; and in a few years, not only were all the expenses met, but there was a good sum over.

After this time the life of Franklin becomes closely united to the STORY OF OUR COUNTRY; so I shall have to leave him for the present, and tell you something about the troublesome times that were coming to the colonies.

XVI.

WHAT HAPPENED TO AN ENGLISH GENERAL.

MOTHER. — We must keep in mind that the French owned Canada.

LIZZIE. — And the English owned what is now the United States.

MOTHER. — At first England claimed the land quite across the country, from the Atlantic to the Pacific. But as the settlements were all along the coast, — not extending into the interior, — the French began to say to themselves, "The English really own only what they have settled; we will explore the western country for ourselves." And some of their adventurers discovering the Mississippi, sailed down that great river till they reached the Gulf of Mexico. After this France claimed all the country watered by the Mississippi or its branches.

WILL. — Wait a minute, please, and let me find it on the map.

MOTHER. — You will see what a large tract of country the French now claimed.

WILL. — Why, yes; there is the Ohio River, which

flows into the Mississippi. Did they claim the country around that?

MOTHER. — They did.

WILL. — See here! If the French claimed all the land watered by this great river and its branches, the English could have only the land east of the Alleghanies.

MOTHER. — That is so. And one of the governors sent word home that if the French were allowed to go on, "the kings of England would not have a hundred miles away from the sea anywhere." England did not take much notice of this at first; and the French went on planning and working, till they had built a chain of forts, sixty in number, reaching from Quebec to New Orleans. This was to show that all the interior of the country belonged to them.

WILL. — I should have thought the English king had better wake up and do something, if he cared anything about his colonies. Just think! He had given up the great fort of Louisburg; so, of course, the French could keep the English from going up the St. Lawrence; and if they had forts on the Mississippi, the English couldn't go up that river either.

MOTHER. — True. And the French said, "If we can keep these two great rivers to ourselves, we shall get most of the American trade into our own hands. The people of the West Indies will be very glad to send their goods up the Mississippi; and we can open trade, too, with all the Indians west of the Alleghanies."

WILL. — But what were the colonies doing all this time? Why didn't they try to get some of the trade?

MOTHER. — The leading men in all the colonies began to be very anxious; and they were glad when the English government advised the colonies to get the Indians to join them against the French. So the colonies each sent a man to Albany to make a treaty for this purpose with a large body of Indians in and around New York, called the "Six Nations." The treaty was made, and the Six Nations promised to help the colonists.

It was hoped, too, that the assembly at Albany would find out the best ways for the colonies to defend themselves in the coming danger.

WILL. — I guess I know what man Pennsylvania sent, — Franklin.

MOTHER. — Yes; and no man did so much good there as he. His advice to the Assembly was something like this: —

"There is very little use in each colony's trying by itself to fight the enemy. The thirteen colonies ought to work together. They ought to be united, as brothers and sisters. If the French, in attacking one settlement, feel that all the rest will rush to the rescue, they will not be so bold in their insults."

LIZZIE. — Did Franklin want all the settlements to become one colony?

MOTHER. — Not at all. He wanted each colony to take care of its own affairs; but also to help all the rest in case of need.-

WILL. — I should think that was a good plan. Didn't the men at Albany think so?

MOTHER. — They were much pleased with this idea of Franklin's; but neither the colonies nor the king liked it. The colonies were afraid it would give too much power to the king; and the king was afraid it would give too much power to the people. So, although the colonies agreed to help each other in case of war, they took no more of Franklin's advice at that time.

A few years before, a number of men in Virginia and Maryland, by the aid of a wealthy London merchant, had obtained a very large grant of land from King George II. This land was in the Ohio valley; and the men called themselves the Ohio Company. Their plan was to form settlements at once, and open a fur trade with the Indians.

WILL. — If George II. and the French king both

said their people might settle there, then there would be another fight between the French and English, I know.

MOTHER. — Yes. And it commenced in this way : The Ohio Company went out to survey the land around the Ohio River. But the French officers who were there told them that the land belonged to France, and no Englishman had a right there. Upon this, the governor of Virginia sent George Washington, then a young man of twenty-one, to say to the French commander that George II. had given the Ohio Company the right to settle the land. But the messenger was received with contempt; the English surveyors were driven away; and the horrors of another war seemed hanging over the colonies.

In 1755, England sent over General Braddock with two regiments, —

WILL. — Then they really began to have war.

MOTHER. — Not just yet. As the troubles were mostly confined to the Ohio valley, it was thought that two thousand English soldiers could easily rout the French, so that the Ohio Company could go on with their work.

General Braddock marched to Frederictown, Maryland, where he waited to collect teams for carrying provisions and other necessaries.

Take your maps, and find Frederictown; and also

11

find Pittsburgh, which is the place General Braddock aimed at. There was a large fort there; and the place was then called Fort Du Quesne. You notice that it stands at the head of the Ohio valley.

WILL. — Yes; two rivers meet there — the Alleghany and Monongahela.

MOTHER. — They unite to form the Ohio.

WILL. — Of course the French would think a great deal of that place.

MOTHER. — While General Braddock was waiting at Frederictown, Franklin was sent to him to say that the colony of Pennsylvania was ready to help him in case of need. Just as he was about to leave, Braddock's agent came back, saying he could get only twenty-five wagons, and some of them were poor.

"Twenty-five wagons!" exclaimed Braddock; "we need a hundred and fifty at least. What miserable business it was to send us over to this country, that is too poor to furnish us a few wagons!"

"You should have sent to Pennsylvania," said Franklin, quietly; "nearly every farmer there keeps a wagon."

"Look here!" said Braddock; "you are known all through the colony: why can't you get us the wagons?"

"Very well," said Franklin; "put in writing what

you need, and what you are willing to pay, and I will try to serve you."

WILL. — General Braddock got his wagons, I know.

MOTHER. — In a few days one hundred and fifty wagons and twenty-one hundred horses arrived at the English camp. Besides these, came a lot of supplies — a present from the Pennsylvania government. All this was through Franklin's influence. Afterwards a number of soldiers from the colonies joined Braddock, George Washington being one of the aids.

LIZZIE. — With so much help General Braddock ought to succeed.

MOTHER. — One would think so. But the English general had too much confidence in himself. Talking of his plans to Franklin one day, he said, —

"The taking of Fort Du Quesne will cost us only three or four days; and then I shall march to Niagara, and after taking that, I shall go to Frontenac."

To this Franklin modestly replied, "To be sure, sir, if you arrive at Fort Du Quesne with all these fine troops! In my mind, your chief danger will be from the Indians, who never fight openly. If large numbers of them hide behind the trees, I am afraid they will surprise your long line of soldiers, and cut it into pieces like a thread."

Braddock smiled confidently, and said, "These

savages may indeed be terrible to your American
militia; but to the king's finely trained soldiers it is
impossible they should do any harm."

WILL. — That's a good joke! General Braddock
didn't know what he was talking about.

MOTHER. — The English soldiers were soon on
their march; but before they even saw the enemy,
they were fired upon from the forests. Seven hundred English soldiers soon lay dead on the field;
and the commander himself, after having five horses
shot under him, was finally carried off with a deadly
bullet in his side.

The English troops were so surprised by the yells
and fighting of the Indians, that it seemed for a time
as if the whole army would be left dead on the field.
But young Colonel Washington came to the rescue.
An Indian chief singled him out to kill him, and
told his warriors to do the same. Two horses were
shot under him; his coat was pierced with four bullets, but he was unharmed. He showed such bravery
that an English officer afterwards said of him, " he
acted as if he really loved the whistling bullets."

Young Washington rallied the raw militia, and
thus the army was saved from destruction.

WILL. — Were the French fighting? and did they
lose many men?

MOTHER. — Of the four or five hundred French

and Indians together, only thirty men and three officers were killed, and thirty wounded.

LIZZIE. — If General Braddock had five horses shot under him, he must have been a brave man. Did he die?

Braddock's Defeat.

MOTHER. — He was silent all day, after being carried from the battle-field; and at night he said, "Who would have thought it?" The next day he said, "We shall know better how to deal with them another time!" — and died.

Upon his death, the command of the army came to Colonel Dunbar, who had been left a few miles back with the provisions and a large body of soldiers in reserve. When the runaways from the battle reached the camp, they so terrified Colonel Dunbar and his men, that the whole body of soldiers — over one thousand — instead of going on to meet the enemy, destroyed all the provisions, that they might have the horses for their own use; then, mounting, with Colonel Dunbar at their head, they galloped from the noise of battle, and could not be persuaded to stop till they were safe in Philadelphia.

WILL. — Brave English troops! Raw American militia!

MOTHER. — Franklin afterwards said that it taught the colonists a good lesson, which was, that they must not think too highly of the bravery of English troops.

LIZZIE. — I should say so!

XVII.

DRIVEN INTO EXILE.

MOTHER. — During the year 1755, the English made another attack on the French, which I am sorry to say was a success.

WILL. — Why do you say you are sorry, when we don't want the French to have America?

MOTHER. — Hear the story, and then see. Do you remember what Nova Scotia used to be called?

WILL. — Acadia; and it was settled by the French before John Smith came over.

MOTHER. — At the time of Braddock's defeat it had about sixteen thousand inhabitants. The Acadians were a simple, hard-working people. The pastures were filled with their flocks. The fertile lands around the many rivers were covered with rich grass and waving wheat. The houses clustered together, and were comfortably furnished. Probably there was not at that time a happier settlement in America. The English were jealous of it. They wanted the fertile fields and the rivers abounding in fish. They wanted control of the fishing-trade on the coasts. So the British government advised the colonies to make an attack on Acadia.

LIZZIE. — Did the Acadians ever trouble the English, as those French people near the Ohio did?

MOTHER. — Never. They had even promised not to join with the French in war; but they had also said they would not fight against France. It was not easy to go to war against a people that would not fight; but the Acadians must be expelled from the country.

The English hit upon a plan. A proclamation was made, commanding old men, young men, and boys of ten years to meet together. Suspecting nothing, they obeyed, not bringing their weapons even. What was their horror to hear this: —

"Henceforth your lands, your houses, and your cattle belong to the king of England. You with your wives and children must all leave the country!"

In a few days the whole people were driven to the sea-shore. A part were hurried on board the few ships waiting for them, and set sail, never again to see their long-loved homes. Those who waited for the return of the ships wandered up and down the shore, or fled to the forests, hungry and half clothed. Children lost their parents, wives their husbands, brothers their sisters.

LIZZIE. — But where did the people who were driven on board the ships go to?

Acadians moving their Household Goods to the Sea-shore.

MOTHER. — They were scattered along the shore from New Hampshire to Georgia.

WILL. — If I had been put ashore, I would have found my way back home again.

MOTHER. — The English thought of that. And while the innocent people who were left behind were wandering up and down the sea-shore, now watching for the return of the ships that had carried away their dear ones, and now casting loving glances toward their hard-earned homes, they saw flames burst forth from the deserted villages. What could it mean? Had some careless villager forgotten his cottage hearth?

Soon the cruel truth dawned upon the sorrowing ones. The English, fearing that the exiles might seek their homes again, after the soldiers had left the neighborhood, had set fire to every homestead in Acadia. The cattle and fields of wheat they had kept for themselves.

LIZZIE. — O, mother! you never told us anything so cruel and so sad.

WILL. — I don't see what excuse the English could have had for such meanness.

MOTHER. — The only possible excuse was that, in 1713, in settling some troubles with France, this little province of Acadia was made over to the English. But the people had been allowed to remain undisturbed, and to have officers of their own choosing.

WILL. — But all that didn't make it right to drive the poor Acadians from their homes.

MOTHER. — It seems as if people's eyes were blinded in times of war, so that they cannot tell right from wrong. There might have been many who felt sorry for the poor exiles; but the English government rejoiced that it had possession of the country bordering on the St. Lawrence.

XVIII.

THE FRENCH AND INDIAN WAR.

MOTHER. — As I have already told you, there had been fighting between the French and English in America for over a year. But England did not really declare war against France till 1756.

The plans for this war were made in England, and the different colonies had to give their help. It was called the French and Indian war. During two years, the English met with shameful losses; and it seemed for a time as if the French would have everything their own way. But a new man came into power in England, named William Pitt. His influence in directing affairs in America was like a mighty river that carries everything before it. But rivers become great through the other rivers which flow into them; and so it was with regard to William Pitt. He learned from Benjamin Franklin what were America's greatest needs.

LIZZIE. — Why! was Franklin in England?

MOTHER. — Yes; he had been sent there by the Pennsylvania government, to lay before the king certain petitions for the welfare of the colony. To be sure, Franklin did not see Pitt; but he frequently saw his two secretaries, who reported to Pitt all he said.

Franklin showed the great need of colonizing the West, especially the country near the Ohio. He also showed that there never could be a lasting peace till Canada belonged to England. And he even planned certain attacks, which were afterwards successfully made.

WILL. — What a great man Franklin was! The last time you spoke of him, he was doing something to help all the colonies. Now he is planning to help England herself.

MOTHER. — Of course the English were anxious to get possession of the forts, especially the most important ones.

WILL. — Then I should think they would have tried to get Louisburg again.

MOTHER. — They did; and in the following year it fell into their hands.

LIZZIE. — And didn't the English get the fort that Braddock tried for?

WILL. — You mean Fort Du Quesne.

MOTHER. — Yes; during this same year the French lost that stronghold. The taking of this fort was a great event in the history of the colonies, for a highway was then opened to the great West, which was never afterwards closed. Washington became famous through his important services at that time. The name of the fort was changed to Pittsburgh, in honor of William Pitt, who planned the expedition.

From this time the English were everywhere successful. Ticonderoga and Crown Point, the two large forts at the head of Lake Champlain, came into the hands of the English; and after these, Niagara.

WILL. — I have found all those places on the map, and it seems to me that if the French had lost Louisburg, Nova Scotia, Ticonderoga, Crown Point, Niagara, and Fort Du Quesne, they couldn't expect to hold out much longer. They couldn't stop the English from going almost anywhere they pleased after that.

MOTHER. — The only very important fort left to the French was at Quebec.

LIZZIE. — I see where Quebec is. It is on the St. Lawrence River.

MOTHER. — And is the most important city on the river. There was a very large fort there, commanded by General Montcalm.

LIZZIE. — He was the French general then — wasn't he?

MOTHER. — Yes; and he had taken such great pains to guard the city carefully at every point, that he thought the English could not possibly get possession of it.

General Wolfe, a brave young officer, had been chosen to make the attack on Quebec. At first the task seemed a discouraging one. The fort itself is on a high point of land overlooking the city; and Wolfe's troops were on the river-side below. Indian spies were watching them from every point; and their every movement was quickly made known to the French commander. After several useless attempts to take it, Wolfe moved his army to a place several miles above the city. One day, as he was riding about to examine the country, he noticed just above Quebec some high cliffs rising abruptly from the river, and at the top of the cliffs a level spot, which he afterwards learned was called the Plains of Abraham. General Montcalm had not guarded this place, for he thought it impossible for any one to scale the steep cliffs. But Wolfe's quick eye detected a little cove, from which a narrow path wound up the steep. Instantly he was on his way back to the camp; and soon all his troops were quietly getting ready to move.

At one o'clock at night, the British army in boats glided quietly down the river, aided by the rapid current of the stream. Darkness hung over them like a curtain. No man was allowed to speak, under

penalty of death.   The little pathway was reached.
Wolfe leaped first on shore.   Encouraged by his
cheerfulness of manner, the men followed their
brave young leader
up the rough ascent.
At sunrise the Brit-
ish army stood on
the Plains of Abra-
ham.

WILL. — How as-

Wolfe's Army ascending the Heights.

tonished General Montcalm
must have been when he saw
the English troops!

MOTHER. — The battle com-
menced at ten o'clock; and after a fierce struggle
the English gained the day.

Before the battle was over, General Wolfe was fatally wounded, and was borne from the field. While dying, he heard the cry, "They run! they run!" Rousing himself, he said, "Who run?" Upon being told it was the French, he said, "I die content!"

Montcalm, too, was mortally wounded. When told he could not survive, he said, "I am glad of it! I shall not live to see the surrender of Quebec!"

WILL. — With both generals gone, there could not be much more fighting.

MOTHER. — No; after the first day of battle, most of the French were willing to give up. The citizens of Quebec said, "We have cheerfully sacrificed our fortunes and our houses, but we cannot expose our wives and children to a massacre." And soon after, the city of Quebec passed into the hands of the English.

This victory of 1759 caused great rejoicing throughout the colonies. ·

There was no more fighting in America at this time; but there were battles upon the sea between the English and French ships.

It was very difficult for the two countries to decide what each should keep or give up. So it was not until 1763 that matters were finally settled and peace declared.

Through the French and Indian war, France lost all her possessions in America, except twenty-three small islands, which she kept as a shelter for her fishermen.

LIZZIE. — Then after 1763 England owned Canada and all the country east of the Mississippi.

WILL. — Quite a big slice for the king to add to his land in America!

XIX.

WASHINGTON'S BOYHOOD.

WILL. — Are you not going to tell us a story about Washington?

LIZZIE. — We did hear about him, in the taking of Fort Du Quesne.

WILL. — Yes; but I want to know about him when he was a little boy, and afterwards too.

MOTHER. — There is not much to be told about him, except as he was working with and for his country; for he went into public service at nineteen. But I will tell you the story.

Washington was born in Virginia in 1732 —

WILL. — Then he was twenty-six years younger than Franklin, for he was born in 1706.

MOTHER. — His father died when he was eleven, leaving quite a large property to the mother, who was to have the management of it till the five children came of age, when it was to be divided between them.

WILL. — Then Washington didn't have to work for a living.

MOTHER. — You are mistaken. The mother was a very wise and energetic woman; and she taught the children to be prudent, economical, and industrious, as she was herself. There were very few schools at the south at that time; so Washington had not the means of getting such a good education as most boys can to-day. His book-learning did not go beyond reading, writing, arithmetic, book-keeping, and surveying.

LIZZIE. — If he went into the army so young, of course he couldn't study much by himself, as Franklin did.

MOTHER. — No; but whatever he undertook was done thoroughly; and some of his school-books show to-day how carefully he wrote, and with what exactness he kept his accounts. He was fond of the study of surveying; and he took great pleasure in making and drawing plans, which he did in the neatest manner. He enjoyed out-door sports, and took every sort of exercise that would increase his strength. Once, it is said, he threw a stone across the Rappahannock opposite his father's house; and no one else was ever known to do it. One of his favorite amusements was playing soldier; and as he seemed to know much more about it than the other boys, they always made him captain.

He was very fond of horses; and one day, mounting a fierce animal that had never been ridden before, undertook to tame him. The horse was a valuable one, belonging to his mother. Washington nearly broke his own neck; but he did not give up. Finally the proud animal burst a blood-vessel, and fell dead beneath his young rider.

WILL. — I guess the mother would rather some one else should tame her horses after that.

MOTHER. — She was very sorry to lose so valuable a horse; but she forgot her loss in the pleasure she felt at having her son come to her at once, and frankly tell her what had happened.

Love of truth was one of Washington's earliest traits of character; and there was not a boy among his school mates who didn't believe that if he said a thing he meant it, or, if he made a promise, he would keep it.

WILL. — I remember a story about Washington, when he was a little boy. Some one made him a present of a new hatchet. He wanted to see how it would cut, so he went and hacked one of his father's cherry trees. When his father came into the orchard, and saw the bark all hacked up, he said, "Who has cut my cherry tree that I thought so much of?" Washington went right up to him and said, "Father, I can't tell a lie; I cut it with my hatchet."

LIZZIE. — Wasn't that noble?

MOTHER. — Washington's oldest brother, Laurence, was a captain in the English navy. When at home, he told stories of his adventures, which so excited George that he was seized with a longing to enter the navy and go to sea. His brother encouraged this; and finally his mother very reluctantly gave her consent. A situation was procured for him, and his clothes were packed and sent on board the ship; but at the last moment the mother felt that he *must not* go, and she begged him to give up all thought of it. Washington dearly loved his mother, and the thought of giving her pain was harder to bear than to give up his longing for the sea. He yielded to her wishes, and staid at home.

WILL. — Lucky he didn't go! What would the country have done without him?

MOTHER. — When he was sixteen, an English nobleman, who owned immense tracts of land in America, was visiting at a neighboring mansion; he became much interested in Washington, and employed him to survey his lands. This occupied Washington for over three years, and was a great advantage to him in many ways. Not only did he receive handsome pay, but he became thoroughly acquainted with the country that Braddock's army afterwards had to pass through.

LIZZIE. — Then that was the reason he was of so much help to General Braddock.

WILL. — He must have had a rough time, out in that wild country.

MOTHER. — Yes, indeed; but he loved to meet hardships; and it was probably the best training he could possibly have had, to fit him for the soldier's life he was afterwards to lead.

WILL. — I can see now why the Virginia government should choose him to carry the message to the French officers on the Ohio: he knew the way, and must have been acquainted with the Indians.

LIZZIE. — And the governor knew that whatever he set out to do, he did well.

MOTHER. — We have now reached the time in his life when he was appointed colonel under General Braddock. After this there is little to tell which you will not hear as I go on with the STORY OF OUR COUNTRY.

LIZZIE. — Was he ever married?

MOTHER. — Yes; when he was twenty-seven he married a beautiful and accomplished young widow, who had two interesting children. When he was not in public service, he lived quietly with his family at his beautiful home on the Potomac, known as Mount Vernon. He was fond of agriculture, and did much to beautify and enrich his lands.

Washington loved little children; and in his later years adopted two of his wife's grandchildren, on the death of their father.

XX.

ANGER AT THE MOTHER COUNTRY.

WILL. — Whenever mother tells us about a great man, I expect to hear about troubles and wars.

LIZZIE. — I don't see how there could be any such things now. Mother said they had no more Indian wars at this time, and no more quarrels with the French.

MOTHER. — The next vexation came from the king himself — George III.

LIZZIE. — What! when all the colonies belonged to him!

WILL. — When John Smith and the other James-town settlers first came over, they had a great bother because James II. was afraid they would forget they all belonged to him. And I can see how this king might annoy the colonies in the same way, if he chose to.

MOTHER. — You have got at a part of the truth. While the settlements remained small, England took little notice of them; but when they grew so that each had a trade of its own, the English government began to be jealous, and said, " The colonies go on choosing their own governors and increasing their trade, as if they had forgotten they belonged to us."

WILL. — But they had charters from the king, which gave them a right to govern themselves.

MOTHER. — After a while these charters were taken away, and the king appointed the governors.

WILL. — I shouldn't think the colonies would have liked that very well.

MOTHER. — Connecticut never gave up her charter. Sir Edmund Andros, who had been appointed governor of New England and New York, went into the assembly at Hartford, and said, " This meeting is not lawful. *I* am governor of Connecticut; and in the king's name I demand the charter of this colony."

The charter lay upon the table. Suddenly the members of the assembly put out all the lights; and one of their number quickly carried out the charter, and hid it in the hollow of a large oak.

WILL. — Good! I wish all the assemblies had done so.

MOTHER. — The next vexation to the colonies came soon after the close of the French and Indian war.

WILL. — Which was in 1763.

MOTHER. — England owed a great deal of money

on account of this war; and she said, "This war was partly for the sake of the colonies, and they ought to help us pay off our great debt."

WILL. — I don't believe England cared so much to help the colonies as to whip France. Besides, I should like to know if the colonies hadn't done their part already. They had sent their men to war; and didn't that cost something?

LIZZIE. — They had all the fighting near their own homes.

MOTHER. — They had suffered much through the war, and they, as well as England, owed a great deal of money on account of it.

WILL. — Then I hope they didn't help England pay off *her* debt.

MOTHER. — The way the king intended to get money from them was by making them pay for the privilege of receiving goods from the English markets. We call such money "duties." The king sent over officers to search the ships coming into port, lest the people should receive goods without paying not alone what they were worth, but the duties also.

When the people heard of this, they were surprised and vexed. They said, "Do not the colonies belong to the king? And shall a man pay for eating bread in his own house? We will have no more goods from England! We will spin and weave for ourselves! And we will eat no more mutton, for fear we shall not have wool enough for our winter clothes!"

WILL. — I am glad the colonists were so spunky! Served the king right!

MOTHER. — Then came another grievance, still worse. The colonists had been very industrious; factories had sprung up along the rivers; and in many of the little towns the busy hum of labor could be heard. Every year were made quantities of linen and woollen cloths, hats, paper, shoes, furniture, and farming tools.

England said, "This manufacturing by the colonists is hurting our trade. They must stop their factories, and buy of us."

And for fear they would go on making things for themselves, England said, "The Americans shall pay us duties on all goods carried from one colony to another."

WILL. — O, how angry that makes me!

MOTHER. — The next vexation they had to bear came through the Stamp Act.

LIZZIE. — What was that?

MOTHER. — No American could buy a newspaper unless it had a stamp on it. And stamps must be bought for all paper used in business. These stamps cost more or less, according to the business they were used in; and often one had to pay a large sum for them. The money paid was all to go to England.

WILL.—The colonists wouldn't stand that, I am sure.

MOTHER. — When the news first reached America, the people were again very indignant. "Does England want to make slaves of us?" they asked. "Shall we give up all our rights as Englishmen? Never!"

There was a young lawyer in Boston, named James Otis, who was a very fine speaker. And when the people met to talk about the Stamp Act, he spoke so grandly and fearlessly that all Boston was on fire with indignation at the injustice; and they said, "We will never be taxed by England! We will not buy a stamp!"

After this, Otis and some other noted men sent letters to the different colonies, begging them *never* to submit to taxation. This was hardly necessary, for they were all angry at England.

In Virginia another eloquent man named Patrick Henry roused the people in the same way.

Some of Otis's writings went over to England; and the king said, "The man is mad! Do not the colonies belong to *us?* Have we not a right to do by them as we choose?"

In the mean time the principal men of this country got together, and agreed to be united by one thought — not to be imposed upon by England. They sent a petition to the king, asking that he would not require them to obey the Stamp Act. They also asked him if a few men might go to parliament to speak for the interest of the colonies. They had a right to expect this; for parliament is made up of men from the different parts of England, each one to speak for the town or county to which he belongs.

WILL. — Then of course they ought to have had men from the colonies in parliament.

MOTHER. — The king took no notice of the petition; and the 1st of November came, the day when the stamps were first to be used. It was set aside as a day of mourning. The bells were muffled and tolled. The flags were at half-mast. The stamp officers were insulted, and their property destroyed. In Boston, a stuffed image of the principal stamp officer was hung by the neck on an elm tree.

For a few days all business which required stamps was stopped. But soon the people concluded to take no notice of the new law, and went on trading as before.

WILL. — I suppose the king didn't like that.

MOTHER. — No; he was more determined than ever to oppress the colonies.

LIZZIE. — Franklin helped the Americans before; couldn't he do something for them now?

MOTHER. — He was in England at this time. He had been chosen by our people to speak of the wrongs they were suffering.

The Stamp Act was displeasing to many in England, as well as in America. The manufacturers and tradesmen were sending in petitions to have it repealed, because they were suffering from the loss of American trade. There was a great talk in parliament as to whether the act ought to be set aside or not.

Franklin was better known and more highly thought of at that time than any other American. Parliament sent for him. And before a crowded house of eager listeners, he was asked all kinds of questions about the colonies. His clear and ready answers, and his description of affairs in this country, had great influence. What he said was thought so important that it was translated into French, and was soon read by all Europe.

LIZZIE. — Then didn't parliament take back the Stamp Act?

MOTHER. — Yes; but I think that even Franklin would not have been able to bring this about, if there had not been one man in parliament who was a friend to the common people everywhere. On that account he was sometimes called the Great Commoner. You heard of him during the French and Indian war.

WILL. — Do you mean William Pitt?

MOTHER. — Yes. Pitt was a very eloquent speaker, and he pleaded hard for the Americans. Among other things, he said: " The colonists ought not to be taxed without their consent. They ought not to be taxed, unless parliament is willing to have some of their chosen men among its members. The Stamp Act is a wicked law, and I am glad the colonies did not obey it."

LIZZIE. — Why wouldn't they have Americans in parliament?

MOTHER. — Franklin said, it was because the English aristocracy, or rich people, felt above the colonists. At any rate, the rich folks didn't like Pitt's speeches, and the poor folks did.

Finally, as I said, the Stamp Act was done away with. The news was joyfully received in America, and great honor was given to the name of Pitt.

LIZZIE. — And not to Franklin?

MOTHER. — Yes, and to Franklin.

XXI.

STIRRING TIMES IN BOSTON.

MOTHER. — The joy felt by the Americans when the Stamp Act was repealed did not last long. The king was more afraid than ever that the colonies would not show proper obedience to his laws. So he sent over a large body of soldiers, under General Gage, to keep the people in awe. Orders also came that these troops were to be housed and fed by the colonists themselves.

WILL. — I guess people didn't relish that!

MOTHER. — New York and Massachusetts refused to care for the troops. Upon this, the Massachusetts governor, who had been appointed by the king, opened the State House for the soldiers; and large numbers of them were in tents on Boston Common.

These English soldiers were very insulting to the citizens, who became more and more alarmed for their rights. Even the children found reason to complain.

13

LIZZIE. — I should think they would have liked to see the soldiers marching about.

MOTHER. — At first they did; for the soldiers had bright red coats, and made a very gay appearance.

Boston Boys standing up for their Rights.

But after a while the Boston boys became much vexed at the red-coats, because they would trample down their forts of snow which they had built on the Common. They asked the soldiers, "What's the use of spoiling our fun?" But the red-coats answered, "Help yourselves if you can, you young rebels!"

Then the boys complained to the captain, but only got laughed at. Finally the little company marched to General Gage himself.

"Who taught you rebellion, and sent you here to show it?" said he.

"No one sent us," said the boys. "We have come to complain of your troops. This is the third time they have spoiled our forts and broken our skating-ice, and we will bear it no longer!"

"Liberty is in the very air, and the boys breathe it!" said General Gage aside to one of his officers. Then to the young soldiers he said, "Go, my brave boys! and take my word for it; if my troops ever trouble you again, they shall be punished."

Shortly afterwards a most serious trouble arose through these same British troops, called the BOSTON MASSACRE.

LIZZIE. — Massacre? That means killing people — doesn't it?

MOTHER. — Yes. One moonlight night, a party of wild young men came down one of the Boston streets. As they drew near the English sentinel who was pacing to and fro in front of the customhouse, he halted, pointed his bayonet towards their breasts, and said in a gruff voice, " Who goes there ? "

The young Bostonians felt they had a right to walk in their own streets, without being stopped by a British red-coat; so they made a rude reply. This provoked the sentinel, and a quarrel began. Other soldiers, who were in the barracks near by, heard the noise and ran out to assist their comrade.

By this time, a good many Bostonians rushed out to see what the fuss was all about. The crowd, which was fast becoming larger, saw that there was a dispute between the British soldiers and the citizens. This was enough to stir them up. They remembered how often the British troops had insulted them, and how patiently they had borne it. Now they were threatening the lives of Massachusetts men. This was past endurance; and they took up snow and lumps of ice and pelted the red-coats. Of course this made the soldiers still more angry.

The noise now reached the ears of the captain. He ordered a squad of soldiers to take their muskets and follow him. They marched through the crowd, roughly pushing people aside, till they reached the sentinel's post. Here the captain drew them up in a semicircle, facing the crowd. When the people saw this, their rage was almost beyond bounds.

" Fire, you lobster-backs ! " yelled some.

" You dare not fire, you cowardly red-coats ! " cried others.

Upon this, the eyes of the soldiers glared upon the people like hungry blood-hounds. The captain waved his sword. The red-coats pointed their guns at the crowd. In a moment the flash of their muskets lighted up the street; and eleven New England men fell bleeding upon the snow: three were dead, and eight wounded.

LIZZIE. — Eleven New England men !

WILL. — The colonists were not any more ready to love George III. after that.

MOTHER. — People throughout the country never forgot that day. A spark was kindled in the hearts of Americans that afterwards grew into a mighty fire.

Not long after the Stamp Act was repealed, the king said, " It will not do to take away every tax on goods sent to America. That will be yielding too much. But we will require them to pay a small amount only, say a few cents on each pound of tea. Surely they will not refuse to pay that ! "

LIZZIE. — I shouldn't think they would have minded just a few cents.

WILL. — But, don't you see? The colonists wouldn't pay any taxes, unless they could send men to parliament.

LIZZIE. — Then the tea tax would make another stir.

MOTHER. — When the news reached the colonies, every true-hearted American declared he wouldn't touch a cup of tea till the tax was taken off.

A large quantity of tea was shipped to South Carolina. The citizens allowed it to be landed, but quietly stored it in damp cellars, where it soon spoiled.

The vessels which brought tea to New York and Philadelphia were compelled to take their cargoes back to England.

Three ships came to Boston laden with tea, which the governor said must be landed. The citizens held indignation meetings in Faneuil Hall. A very daring man, who dearly loved his country, and was ready to die for her, took the lead in these meetings. His name was Samuel Adams. The English hated him, because he stirred up the people to a love of liberty.

During one of these meetings, a petition was sent to the governor, asking permission to have the tea carried back to England. The answer came to the waiting crowd that the tea must be landed. Then Samuel Adams rose and said, " This meeting can do nothing more to save the country."

Instantly a war-whoop was heard at the entrance

of the hall; and a party of fifty men, disguised as Indians, rushed down to the wharf, jumped on board the ships, and threw every chest of tea overboard.

WILL and LIZZIE. — Hurrah for Boston!

MOTHER. — This was in 1773; and it was called "The Boston Tea Party."

XXII.

THE QUARREL INCREASES.—FIGHTING BEGINS.

MOTHER.—When the news of these events reached England, the king said, "Boston shall be punished for this;" and an order was given forbidding any ship to go to Boston, even from American ports.

WILL.—Then how could the people get what they needed?

MOTHER.—The ships were to go to Salem. But the Salem people would not take advantage of the Boston Port Bill, as it was called. They freely invited the Boston merchants to come there and use their wharves.

Parliament knew that Massachusetts would rebel; for the people of Boston suffered greatly from this sudden losing of their trade. So four thousand more soldiers were sent to Massachusetts, and General Gage, commander of the British troops in America, was appointed governor of the colony.

WILL.—If Massachusetts couldn't help herself, the other colonies would do something for her, I know.

MOTHER. — They sent a great many gifts to Massachusetts. The southern colonies sent flour and rice; the middle colonies, corn and iron; and many towns sent money.

LIZZIE. — England didn't expect the Boston folks would be helped in that way, I am thinking.

MOTHER. — The British government thought the Boston Port Bill would frighten the colonies into obedience. But Massachusetts, too indignant to be afraid, resolved that there should be a meeting of the principal men of the colonies to see what could be done to protect themselves against the increasing insults of the mother-country.

WILL. — As the governors of the different colonies were chosen by the king, I can see that they would not like such a meeting as that.

MOTHER. — They did not. But the people were not hindered in their plan; and a meeting was held in Philadelphia, called the FIRST CONTINENTAL CONGRESS. At this congress it was decided that the whole country should help Massachusetts get her rights. They also resolved to send one more petition to the king.

In the mean time the people of Masachusetts had a meeting, at which John Hancock presided.

LIZZIE. — John Hancock — who was he?

MOTHER. — He was a wealthy Boston merchant,

who dared to say or do anything for the good of his country.

At this meeting it was decided to call upon the citizens to form themselves into military companies, who would be ready to take up arms at a minute's warning. On this account they were called Minutemen.

Soon all the other colonies got ready to defend themselves in the same way.

LIZZIE. — Didn't the king treat them any better after he got the petition from the people?

MOTHER. — George III. was stubborn; and the more unwilling the colonists were to obey cruel laws, the more determined he was to take all privileges from them.

The next thing he did was to forbid any New Englanders fishing off the coast of Newfoundland.

WILL. — I don't see what there was left for the colonists to do, but to starve, or fight for their rights. Of course, after they had worked so hard, clearing the forests and fighting the Indians, to get decent homes for themselves, they wouldn't give up everything, to be worse off than they were before they came over.

MOTHER. — They didn't really think of war at this time. They only wanted to get their rights, and not be imposed upon by England.

WILL. — I shouldn't think General Gage would have liked their raising companies of soldiers.

MOTHER. — He did not; and he determined to destroy their military stores, if they should have any.

The colonists suspected this. They had a quantity of powder, muskets, &c., at Concord, about sixteen miles from Boston. As it was feared that General Gage might find it out, there was an understanding that certain citizens should watch the enemy's movements. If at any time English troops should march from Boston, there was to be a signal given from the belfry of the old North Church.

One night, in April, 1775, a thrill of alarm filled a little band of patriots in Charlestown, as they saw a light appear in the belfry. Paul Revere, who had been chosen to carry the news to Concord, quickly mounted a horse; with almost lightning speed he galloped to Medford. Here he stopped at a house where Samuel Adams and John Hancock were sleeping.

"Don't make so much noise!" said a man on guard before the house.

"Noise!" said Paul Revere. "You'll have noise enough before long! The red-coats are on their way to Concord!" And away he flew, giving the alarm at the house of every sleeping farmer till he reached Concord.

WILL.—I am sure there wasn't much more sleeping that night.

MOTHER. — As soon as the Concord people were roused, they began moving the military stores into the woods. In the mean time, eight hundred British troops, under command of Major Pitcairn, were on the road. They had hoped to quietly get possession of the stores before morning. But as they passed along, and heard the ringing of bells, and saw the hurrying to and fro of the people, they knew that their plans had been found out. So they sent back for more troops.

Major Pitcairn reached Lexington, a town east of Concord, at four o'clock in the morning. Here he found seventy minute-men in arms, collected on the green.

"You villains! you rebels!" cried he; "disperse! Why don't you lay down your arms and disperse?"

Then the British soldiers fired, and eighteen of the seventy Lexington men were killed or wounded. Then the red-coats, giving three "hurrahs," marched on towards Concord.

LIZZIE. — O, that was too bad!

WILL. — What else could the Concord soldiers expect, when there were nearly a thousand British?

MOTHER. — On that same morning, — April 19, 1775, — about four hundred and fifty minute-men had assembled on a hill overlooking Concord. From this point they could see the English destroying their military stores and provisions. They saw them cut down the liberty-pole and set the court-house on fire.

WILL. — O, how the Concord men must have longed to let their bullets fly!

MOTHER. — They knew it was useless to attack so much larger numbers in an open fight.

A portion of the English were guarding a bridge at the entrance of the town. The minute-men marched down from the hill, and fired upon these red-coats, who fled in great confusion, having one man killed and several wounded.

When the English had destroyed all the military stores they could find, they set out to return to Boston, carrying their wounded. But they were not to go back as easily as they came.

WILL. — I guess they wouldn't if I had been a minute-man!

MOTHER. — The whole country around was roused, and men came hurrying from all directions. They were generally in their shirt-sleeves, but they had guns in their hands and powder in their flasks. Scarcely a tree or a wall did the English pass that did not shelter minute-men. Sometimes there were companies, sometimes only single farmers. The

English afterwards said, " It seemed as if men dropped from the clouds."

Every mile the British made in their march back, the fewer men did they have.   At last their ammu-

Retreat of the British from Concord.

nition was nearly gone, and they began to run in great disorder.

WILL. — Brave English troops !   Raw country militia !

MOTHER. — Before long, more troops from Boston

came to their aid. These troops formed a hollow square, into which the tired runaways ran, and threw themselves down on the ground for rest, their tongues hanging out of their mouths, like hunted dogs.

During the rest of their march they were constantly fired upon, so that they were glad to get back to Boston, under the protection of General Gage.

If the English had not been re-enforced, they would have had to surrender. As it was, they lost two hundred and seventy-three men; while the Americans lost only eighty-eight.

WILL. — I wonder what George III. said to that!

MOTHER. — England was greatly astonished to hear that the regulars, as the king's troops were called, had retreated or run away from American farmers.

LIZZIE. — I guess the other colonies were surprised when they heard of it too.

MOTHER. — It caused a great excitement all over the country.

When Samuel Adams heard the guns at Lexington, he exclaimed, " What a glorious morning is this ! "

LIZZIE. — Glorious?

MOTHER. — He knew that the time had come when men were to fight for their freedom.

WILL. — And I suppose he knew they could not get it in any other way.

MOTHER. — It seemed to be all that was left for Americans to do; for when George III. heard how affairs were going on, he immediately sent over another large body of troops, under three famous generals, named Howe, Clinton, and Burgoyne: so that there were now ten thousand soldiers in Boston.

In the meantime, Samuel Adams, John Hancock, and other leading men had aroused more Americans to enlist as soldiers, in case they should be attacked by the English; and before the end of April, fifteen thousand men had gathered about Boston.

WILL. — I suppose they didn't know much about war.

MOTHER. — No; and they had very few cannon and muskets, and only a little powder.

LIZZIE. — I hope the English didn't know this.

WILL. — If they knew there were fifteen thousand men around Boston, who were ready to fight, I don't believe they were in a hurry to get outside of the city. They remembered too well the run from Concord.

MOTHER. — General Gage began to get ready for war. The king, George III., had told him to offer pardon to any who would leave the American side and join the English. But there were two men who were not to be pardoned, but were to be hanged if caught.

WILL. — I think I know who they were — Sam Adams and John Hancock. But that shows what true patriots they were.

14

XXIII.

THE REVOLUTIONAY WAR.

MOTHER. — Boston is partly enclosed by two ranges of highlands — Dorchester Heights on the south, and Bunker Hill and Breed's Hill on the north-west. These two hills are in Charlestown. Both parties were anxious to get possession of these ranges.

WILL. — Yes; for the army that was on the hills could keep the other army out of Boston.

MOTHER. — The Americans found out that General Gage was getting ready to move a part of his troops on to the heights in Charlestown; so one night Colonel Prescott was sent with about a thousand men, to throw up banks of earth on Bunker Hill.

LIZZIE. — I don't see what that was for.

MOTHER. — In case the British tried to take the hill, the Americans could hide behind this earth fort, and protect themselves from the attacks of the enemy.

Prescott's soldiers worked so quietly that the English knew nothing of what was going on till the next morning, when they saw the earth fort. Then

General Gage watched the Americans through a telescope, and decided it was best to commence battle at once. He ordered a firing of cannon from Copp's Hill in Boston and from the ships of war in the harbor. The Americans went on with their work, and cared little for the firing. They lost by it only one man.

It was the morning of the·17th of June, 1775. General Gage sent four thousand soldiers to Charlestown in boats. The weather was very hot; and the English troops carried knapsacks on their backs weighing over a hundred pounds each. In the meantime the dreadful news of the coming battle was spread, and every roof in Boston and Charlestown was crowded with people anxiously watching the two sides.

Colonel Prescott and General Putnam were moving about among their soldiers, giving orders and speaking words of cheer, when a handsome young man on horseback came galloping up and said, " I come to aid as a volunteer. Tell me where I can be most useful."

This was General Warren, a physician of Boston, a true patriot, who had given a large part of his time to serving his country since the troubles with England began.

General Putnam exclaimed, " Is it you, General

Warren? I am glad and sorry to see you! Your
life is too precious to be exposed in this battle.
But since you are here, go to the fort; you will
there be covered."

"I came not to be covered," replied General Warren. "Tell me where the battle will be hottest."

"The enemy will try to take the fort," said General Putnam. "If that can be defended, the day is
ours."

General Warren rode along to the fort. The
troops recognized him, and welcomed him with
three cheers, for he was much beloved.

WILL. — You said there were four thousand
British soldiers. Were there only a thousand
Americans to fight them?

MOTHER. — Others had joined them, so that there
were now between two and three thousand. But
they were not nearly so well prepared for battle as
the English. They were without food and water,
and had very little ammunition — by that I mean
powder and balls. But they had the pure fire of
patriotism in their hearts.

After a while the English troops began to move
slowly up the hill, dragging their cannons after
them. The American drums beat to arms. Putnam, who was still at work on the fort, led his men
into action. "Keep still!" said he. "Don't fire

till you see the whites of their eyes; then aim at the officers."

The British troops were now only eight rods off. "Now, men! now is your time!" said Prescott. "Make ready! Take aim! *Fire!*"

The smoke cleared away: the whole hill-side below the fort was covered with the dead; and the remaining English troops were running down the hill.

WILL. — Hurrah for victory!

MOTHER. — Victory had not come yet. After the first attack there was a pause in the battle. It was only the lull that comes before the thunder-bolt. Charlestown was in flames, by order of the British general.

LIZZIE. — How wicked!

MOTHER. — Soon the British troops again ascended the hill. Again they were driven back. Victory for the Americans seemed almost certain. Putnam rode along the line, shouting, " Drive back the redcoats once more, boys, and the day is ours!"

The English soldiers were very unwilling to advance again; but their officers made still greater preparations for the third attack. More troops came over from Boston, and they were ordered to leave their knapsacks behind. General Howe had so arranged his cannon that they would sweep along the whole line of the Americans.

WILL. — And our men hadn't any cannon.

MOTHER. — Scarcely any; and now their powder and balls were almost gone. There was hardly enough for one more round of firing. And when the third attack from the English came, there was nothing to be done but to fire once and then fall back.

LIZZIE. — Too bad!

MOTHER. — In the retreat they lost far more than in the battle. The English finally won the day; but they dearly bought it. They had lost over a thousand men; the Americans not half as many. But among the Americans the bravest of the brave had fallen — the beloved General Warren. When General Howe heard this, he said, " Warren's death is equal to the loss of five hundred men to the Americans."

LIZZIE. — So the Americans got beaten at the battle of Bunker Hill, after all.

WILL. — Not so badly as might be. I don't see how they got along as well as they did — a lot of farmers fighting the king's regulars, who had spent their lives in training for war.

MOTHER. — If this battle was a loss to the Americans in one way, it was a great gain in another. It gave them confidence in themselves, and showed them that the king's troops were not so much to be feared after all. They also learned that the English were determined to oppose them; and they found out for sure that if they would regain the liberties which had been taken from them, they must fight.

When Washington first heard of the battle, he only asked, " Did our men stand fire ? " Being told that they did, and that they waited till the enemy was only eight rods off, he said, " The liberties of the country are safe ! "

WILL. — I should think the battle would have taught the Americans to be better prepared for war.

MOTHER. — Congress took the matter in hand, and voted that a larger army should be raised, consisting of men from all the colonies. Washington was chosen commander-in-chief.

WILL. — That means, I suppose, he was put at the head of the army.

MOTHER. — He left Virginia, and arrived at Cambridge, near Boston, in July, 1775, and was met everywhere with cheers of welcome. Soon after his arrival, Washington, standing under a large elm-tree at Cambridge, in the name of the thirteen colonies took command of the army. He was then forty-three years old, tall, broad-chested, and fine-looking. He was a commander that any army in the world might well be proud of.

WILL. — He must have thought he had come to a queer-looking set, if they didn't look any better than they did at Concord or Bunker Hill.

MOTHER. — Few of the seventeen thousand men whom Washington found waiting for him had any uniform. They had come in their old coats or in their shirt-sleeves. Their muskets were mostly such as they had used in shooting game around their homes; hardly two were alike. But Washington thought of something more than outward appearances. He looked into the faces of these rugged men, and read there a daring and determination which gave him hope and courage.

The first thing he did was to try to bring the army into habits of neatness and regularity. The men had no idea of military discipline, and came and went as they chose. Their friends from the country were constantly visiting them, sometimes to bring clothing and eatables, oftener from curiosity. Washington at once set the men to work. At first this was difficult, and many of the men complained at the new order of things; but their commander's kindness of heart soon made him loved by all.

Washington's greatest cause of anxiety was that they had so little ammunition. He at once wrote to Congress: "Our scarcity of powder is much more alarming than I had the faintest idea of."

LIZZIE. — They couldn't fight any battles right away, then — could they?

MOTHER. — No. Washington knew of the suffering of many patriots in Boston. Between six and seven thousand people were shut up there by the English troops. They had little to eat, and could get no word to or from their friends outside. Washington's plan was to drive the English out of Boston, and relieve these suffering ones. Scarcity of powder forced him to remain quiet many months; but during the next year the army was sufficiently supplied with ammunition to make him feel that he might venture an attack on Boston.

So, in March, 1776 —

WILL. — That was nine months after the battle of Bunker Hill —

MOTHER. — Washington formed a plan for getting his troops on to Dorchester Heights, which you remember is a line of hills on the south of Boston.

WILL. — Wasn't General Gage on the lookout for this?

MOTHER. — General Gage had been recalled to England after the battle of Bunker Hill; and General Howe was in his place. Washington wished to get on to the heights without General Howe's knowing it. In order to do this, he ordered cannons to be fired into the town from the hills around.

LIZZIE. — How the Boston people must have felt to see the cannon-balls coming!

MOTHER. — The English at once commenced firing in return, so that for two or three days there was a great noise.

WILL. — That would give the Americans a good chance to move without being seen, because the smoke from the cannons would make the air so thick.

MOTHER. — On the morning of the 5th of March, the British saw with astonishment the forts which had sprung up as if by magic on Dorchester Heights. General Howe knew that he must then do one of two things — drive the American farmers from the heights, or leave the town.

" If they stay there, I cannot keep a ship in the harbor," said he.

Finally, he concluded to make an attack on the heights. But his men looked pale and uneasy.

WILL. — They remembered Bunker Hill, I guess.

MOTHER. — They wished Boston and all New England at the bottom of the sea, and themselves back in England. When the troops on Dorchester Heights saw the English get into boats and come to attack them, their hearts kindled with joy, for they felt sure they should be victorious.

By Washington's orders they had collected on

top of the heights a large number of barrels filled with earth and stones. These were hidden from view by quantities of hay. The hills were steep and bare, and these heavy barrels were to be rolled down on the enemy, in case they tried to scale the heights. But the farmer-soldiers were disappointed. A violent rain-storm arose, which threw the line of boats into great disorder, and spoiled the ammunition of the English, so that they were compelled to give up all idea of making an attack. Howe then decided to leave Boston at once.

Washington sent word that he would not trouble the departing troops if they would leave the town without injuring it.

LIZZIE. — I suppose he was afraid they might burn it, as they did Charlestown.

MOTHER. — General Howe consented to this arrangement, and set out with his army for Halifax. As soon as they were gone, Washington and his troops entered Boston, amid the shouts and cheers of the people. Every heart was bounding with joy and thankfulness toward the great commander.

LIZZIE. — I hope the red-coats stayed away now, and didn't trouble the colonists any more.

MOTHER. — On the contrary, when the king heard of the disgrace of his troops, he said the colonists must be whipped at any cost. And he sent more troops to America.

Washington felt sure that the English would plan another attack soon. So, fearing that General Howe, on leaving Boston, might steer for New York, he sent a body of troops under General Putnam to protect that place; and soon he himself followed with the rest of his army.

We must leave Washington now for a while, and see what Congress is doing; for, though Washington was at the head of the army, he had to depend much on Congress for advice and help.

I wish I had time to tell you about all the great and good men there were in Congress at that time. I suppose there was not a man who went there for his own gain or pleasure. They said, —

"When the war began, we hoped it would soon be over, for we supposed that England would decide to treat us well. We were proud to feel that we belonged to Great Britain, whose government is the best in the world. How glad we should have been to love, honor, and serve her always. But the king himself has hindered us from doing this. Instead of helping us to be prosperous and happy, he has tried to make us slaves!

"There is only one thing left for us to do — say that we no longer belong to England, that we are now *free states*, and that we will make our own laws, and take care of ourselves, and let George III. help himself if he can."

This was a very daring thing to do; but the best and wisest men in the country thought it the only right course to take.

One of the leading men of Congress — Thomas Jefferson of Virginia — put something like these thoughts on paper. Five men, one of whom was Benjamin Franklin, were chosen to look over each line, and see if it could be made better. This paper was adopted by Congress on the Fourth of July, 1776, and was called THE DECLARATION OF INDE-PENDENCE.

LIZZIE. — Now I know why the Fourth of July is such a great day. It was Our Country's Birthday. Did everybody celebrate the first Fourth of July?

MOTHER. — There was great rejoicing in all the colonies as soon as they knew what had been done. The army around New York was called together by the beating of drums, to listen to the reading of the Declaration of Independence. The soldiers were wild with enthusiasm.

WILL. — They didn't know before exactly what they were fighting for. Now they knew the war wouldn't be finished till George III. gave up that they were free.

LIZZIE. — But I thought they *were* free. They called themselves so.

WILL. — It was one thing to say America was free, and another thing to make it so.

MOTHER. — About this time Congress took another important step. It sent three men, one of whom was Franklin, to France, to see if the French would treat America as a free nation.

WILL. — I don't believe they would.

LIZZIE. — Why not?

WILL. — Because, if they took sides with America, England would go to war against them again.

MOTHER. — That is one reason why the French king was not yet ready to call America a free country. But the French people all hoped England would lose the colonies, and they secretly sent ammunition to help our army. Many French soldiers were sent over too. A young nobleman of twenty, named Lafayette, felt so much sympathy for the Americans that he fitted out a vessel at his own expense, in which he and his companions crossed the ocean. He then offered his services to Congress as a common soldier.

WILL. — Of course they wouldn't let him be a common soldier.

MOTHER. — He was made a general, and soon became a great favorite, not only with Washington but with all who knew him.

Not long after the declaration of independence, our beautiful flag was first used. Look at the picture and count the stripes and stars.

WILL. — There are thirteen stripes.

LIZZIE. — And thirteen stars.

MOTHER. — You can guess why the number of each is just thirteen.

LIZZIE. — Ah, I know! Because there were thirteen colonies.

WILL. — They put more stars on the flag now.

MOTHER. — Yes. Our flag still has thirteen stripes, in memory of the original colonies; but another star is added whenever a new state comes into the Union.

XXIV.

THE WAR GOES ON.

MOTHER. — You remember that Washington left Boston.

WILL. — He went to New York, because he was afraid General Howe would serve that city as he did Boston.

MOTHER. — Washington placed a large number of his troops on Long Island, opposite New York, and the rest were in New York itself.

Several more regiments of British troops were sent over; so that there were now twenty thousand red-coats in America, besides a large fleet of war-vessels.

General Howe attacked the army on Long Island, and defeated it. The Americans lost five times as many men as the English did.

After this Washington, on a dark and foggy night, withdrew his troops to some heights north of New York, called Harlem Heights. Before long he was driven from there, and met the English in battle at White Plains, neither side gaining a victory. Then, learning that the English were intending to go into

New Jersey, he crossed over into that state with most of his troops.

Not long afterwards, he was again beaten by the enemy.

LIZZIE. — What! good, brave Washington so often beaten! I cannot understand it.

WILL. — I do. What else could be expected, when the British had more men, more guns, and more powder?

MOTHER. — During the next few weeks, Washington was driven farther and farther south, till he reached Trenton. There he crossed the Delaware to the Pennsylvania side.

WILL. — The country couldn't have felt much encouraged, to have the army running away so from the red-coats.

MOTHER. — People were much disheartened, and Washington had great cause for anxiety. His soldiers were leaving him by hundreds. And besides, many leading men in New Jersey and Pennsylvania were going over to the English. But, whatever Washington felt, he showed no fear or lack of hope. He knew, however, that some daring attack must soon be made.

Across the river in Trenton there were about a thousand Hessians —

WILL. — Hessians — what were those?

15

MOTHER. — They were troops that England had
hired from Germany. Washington felt sure that on
Christmas day they would be having a grand cele-
bration, so that they would not watch his movements. Therefore the night of the 25th of Decem-

Washington crossing the Delaware.

ber, 1776, would be a good time for him to recross
the Delaware.

It was bitter cold. The river was rapidly freezing. The current, which at that point was very
swift, hurled along masses of ice. The wind blew
fiercely. Some of Washington's officers would not

join him, as they thought it would be impossible for him to reach the other side.

It was twilight when the commander and his troops reached the river's edge. Only a part could cross at a time; and the poor, half-fed, half-clothed men that lingered on the banks shivered in the December cold. At eleven, a blinding snow-storm set in. Would the little army ever reach Trenton?

But Washington had inspired them with the sentiment, Liberty or death! and they pushed on. At three o'clock in the morning, the Americans were all on the Jersey side. In an hour more they started on their silent march. It was nine miles to Trenton, and there were steep hills to climb. At daybreak they reached the little town. The Hessians slept late, for they had not recovered from the revelries of the day before. Fighting for the English, they thought, was not an unpleasant matter after all; they had gay times, and the fare was good.

But suddenly the Hessians were awakened by the beat of drums, and the shouts of the officers, "The Americans are upon us!"

The half-drunken Hessian commander tried to rally his men and bring them into order. Then they set out to make a retreat. But it was too late. The Americans surrounded them. The Hessian commander and forty of his men were killed.

The rest were in terror. What could they do? Where should they go?

They felt their helplessness; and they sent word to Washington that they would surrender. A thousand Hessians, with their guns and cannon, fell into the hands of the Americans, who had lost only four men.

At this good news, Washington, whose strong will had been strained for seventeen hours, gave way for the moment to his feelings. With clasped hands and glistening eyes, he looked up to Heaven in thankfulness.

WILL. — They caught the Hessians; but did they get back safe to the other side?

MOTHER. — Yes, they crossed immediately; for Washington felt sure that the English remaining in New Jersey would attack him when they heard the news; and he was right.

A large number of the regulars under Cornwallis marched to Trenton.

"It will be an easy thing," said the English general, "to surround Washington's army. We will make an attack in the morning."

But when morning came, the American troops were gone, no one knew where; and the next thing Cornwallis heard was that Washington had attacked Princeton, had been victorious, and that the

English had lost four times as many men as the Americans.

The successes at Trenton and Princeton were very cheering to the people everywhere, and the soldiers became more hopeful.

After the battles we have spoken of, Washington did not make any more attacks for several months; but stationed his army so that they could watch the English.

WILL. — And I suppose the English generals were planning how they could pay him off for what they had lost.

MOTHER. — The English had already aimed at Boston and New York. Can you not guess what other large city they wanted?

LIZZIE. — It must have been Philadelphia.

WILL. — Then Washington was determined they shouldn't get it.

MOTHER. — The armies met on the Brandywine, a little river flowing into the Delaware south of Philadelphia. Unfortunately the Americans were beaten; so that General Howe and his large army took possession of Philadelphia.

LIZZIE. — Too bad!

MOTHER. — What made it more trying was that while the king's troops were in such comfortable quarters, enjoying even luxuries, our soldiers were suffering the greatest hardships.

WILL. — Where were they?

MOTHER. — At Valley Forge, about twenty miles from Philadelphia. Washington chose that place for his army to stay in during the winter, because he thought it could be easily defended in case of an attack, and because he could watch the movements of the enemy.

LIZZIE. — Why did the soldiers suffer?

MOTHER. — They had so few of the necessaries of life. Rough huts which they made themselves were all that protected them from the cold winter winds.

WILL. — Well, huts were all the Indians had to live in.

MOTHER. — The Indians had plenty of blankets made of warm furs. These poor soldiers had no blankets. Their clothing was ragged and thin. They had no shoes; so that their marches over the ice and frozen ground could be traced by the bloody tracks of their naked feet. Many a night the groups of soldiers could be seen sitting around their wood fires to keep warm, not daring to go to sleep for fear the intense cold might so benumb them that they would never wake.

Think of lying on the frosty ground without even a blanket to cover one! Even a heap of straw would have been a luxury. They often went without food; and what they had was of the poorest kind.

Yet the soldiers did not complain. They all loved Washington; and they knew he would have helped them to better fare had it been in his power. Perhaps he suffered more than any one else; for his heart was burdened with the needs of all. But the keenest pain to Washington was to feel that the people were dissatisfied because he was not making any attack on the English. The people in Pennsylvania particularly kept sending petitions to Congress to have the enemy driven out of Philadelphia.

WILL. — I can't blame them for wanting to get rid of the red-coats; but they might have known that Washington couldn't do much fighting when his men were half frozen and half starved.

LIZZIE. — I don't see how the country could get free if the army was so badly off.

MOTHER. — Fortunately, not all the army was at Valley Forge. Washington had sent a large portion of his men to the far north.

XXV.

THE AMERICAN CAUSE MORE HOPEFUL.

ENGLAND had made a plan which, if it had been successful, would have hurt the American cause very much   Before I tell you about it, look at your maps and find the St. Lawrence and Lake Champlain.

WILL. — Lake Champlain empties into the St. Lawrence.

MOTHER. — Now tell me what fort is near the head of the lake.

LIZZIE. — I see — Fort Ticonderoga.

WILL. — We ought to remember that, because it was one of the famous forts during the French and Indian war.

MOTHER. — The English had said, " It would be a great thing if we could manage to cut off New England from the rest of the colonies ! In that case they could not hear from Congress, and they could not get any troops from the south. There would be nothing for them to do but to surrender."

WILL. — I tell you, the Yankees wouldn't do that !

MOTHER. — In order to carry out this plan, General Burgoyne was sent up the St. Lawrence with eight thousand regular troops, besides Canadians and Indians. He went up to Lake Champlain.

WILL. — And of course took Fort Ticonderoga.

MOTHER. — From there he was to march to the Hudson, and so push on to New York.

WILL. — I see. If he could do that, New England would be cut off.

MOTHER. — The first thing he did after taking Fort Ticonderoga was to spy out what military stores the Americans had collected in that region. There was a large supply of ammunition at Bennington, Vermont, which Burgoyne was determined to destroy.

When the people of Vermont found this out, they sent a letter to the New Hampshire Assembly, begging for help. And the help was not long in coming. Men came flocking from all directions to save Bennington, as they had done to protect Concord.

Luckily there was an American officer near at the time, who had fought bravely at Bunker Hill, and had been in the thickest of the fights at Trenton and Princeton. His name was Colonel Stark. The English reached Bennington, sure of victory, after which they were going to march into Connecticut and destroy more ammunition.

Colonel Stark rallied about him the brave men who had left their farms at a moment's warning, bringing nothing with them but their muskets. As the British approached for the attack, he called out, —

"There are the red-coats! We must conquer them, or Molly Stark is a widow!"

The New Englanders had a glorious victory. They lost less than one hundred men, while the enemy lost eight hundred.

WILL. — I guess Bennington kept its ammunition.

MOTHER. — Yes; and there was added to it a large quantity of cannon, guns, and powder taken from the English.

This battle crippled General Burgoyne very much; so that he was obliged to wait for more ammunition before he tried again to capture military stores.

WILL. — Pity about that!

MOTHER. — The whole country was alive with excitement. Washington sent many of his best troops, to be ready for another battle, which he knew must soon come. Congress rallied men from all parts of the country to join the northern wing of the army; so that a large number gathered at Saratoga, under command of General Gates.

Find Saratoga on the map.

LIZZIE. — Here it is: in New York, north of Albany, not far from the Hudson River.

MOTHER. — The Americans made several little attacks on different parts of Burgoyne's army; but the final battle came off at Saratoga.

WILL. — Which side beat?

MOTHER. — Burgoyne was completely routed. Instead of pushing down to Albany and eating his Christmas dinner, as he had boasted he would do, he was obliged to surrender. This was a terrible blow to British power in America. Burgoyne had lost, through these battles, since he first landed in Canada, ten thousand men, besides large stores of ammunition.

WILL. — Only think! ten thousand red-coats lost to England!

LIZZIE. — No; they were not all red-coats. There were some Indians and Canadians among them.

MOTHER. — Many of this number were killed, many deserted, but several thousands became prisoners in the hands of the Yankees.

LIZZIE. — How the good news must have cheered Washington!

MOTHER. — It had a wonderful effect, not only giving hope to the suffering troops, but making the whole country rejoice. It also helped the American cause in Europe. Franklin had no difficulty now

in getting a hearing at the French court; and France
signed a treaty, promising help to America, which it
now called a free and independent country.   I doubt
if there was another
man living who could
have done the good
service which Frank-
lin did in this way.

Franklin at the French Court.

WILL. — And what did England say about it all?

MOTHER. — Parliament began to think there was
some truth in what Franklin had said — that if the

Americans once began to fight for their independence, they would never give up till they were free. The English also thought it was time to treat the Americans a little more civilly.

WILL. — Perhaps George III. didn't like the idea of another war with France just then.

MOTHER. — Already many of his people were getting tired of the war with America. Besides, the other countries of Europe began to favor American freedom.

WILL. — And the king wouldn't like to have all Europe in war against him.

MOTHER. — For those reasons, the king sent word to the colonies that they might have all they had asked for before the war began.

WILL. — Rather late to answer their petitions now!

MOTHER. — So the Americans thought; and they sent word back that, although in the beginning they only wanted their rights as English colonists, they would now be satisfied with nothing short of their freedom. And so the war went on.

LIZZIE. — I should think the Americans must have felt very glad when they heard that France would help them.

WILL. — But the English generals wouldn't be very glad!

MOTHER. — As soon as General Howe heard that war-ships were coming over from France, he thought best to leave Philadelphia, and join his other troops near New York, expecting there might be a battle when the French arrived.

LIZZIE. — So if the English *did* get Philadelphia, they had to leave it, as they once left Boston.

WILL. — Where was Washington all this time?

MOTHER. — As soon as he heard that General Howe had left Philadelphia, he followed after; and at Monmouth Court-House there was a battle fought, in which the English lost many more than the Americans. General Howe was glad, when night came on, to silently steal away to New York.

Washington followed him, and stationed his troops so that he could watch the English army.

WILL. — And was there fighting when the French came?

MOTHER. — There were no large battles for a long time. During the next year, the English destroyed many small towns, which did not help their cause very much, nor do any great injury to the Americans.

It seemed as if the English generals were vexed because they had lost so many men in battle, or because the war had lasted so long; and they gave vent to their feelings by constant cruelties. Their excuse was, that they expected in this way to frighten the people into submission to the king.

Will. — A poor way to bring it about!

Mother. — The English lost more than they gained in this way; for every new outrage which the Americans heard of, only made them more determined to fight on for their freedom.

Lizzie. — What states suffered most in this way?

Mother. — Towns were plundered and burned in Massachusetts, Rhode Island, Connecticut, and New Jersey, and many people put to death.

Lizzie. — I don't believe Washington would have let his men do so.

Mother. — He was much opposed to all kinds of needless cruelty, and did everything in his power to make his men kind.

Once, when a party of red-coats made a raid into Connecticut, General Putnam had a chance to show his valor and patriotism. — By the way, do you remember where you first heard of General Putnam?

Lizzie. — I do; at Bunker Hill. He was afraid his men would waste their powder by firing on the enemy too soon. But what were you going to tell us?

Mother. — When he heard that the English were approaching the town of Greenwich, and that they were destroying houses and mills, he gathered about him a few men of the neighborhood, determined to do all in his power to save the town. He had but a hundred and fifty men, while the English had ten times as many. He had two cannons, which he placed on the top of a steep hill. As soon as the enemy came near enough, he fired his cannons.

WILL. — What could a hundred and fifty men do against fifteen hundred?

MOTHER. — Most of the red-coats were on horse-back. When Putnam saw the English dragoons were about to make a charge on them, he ordered his men to flee into a swamp near by, where horses could not enter.

WILL. — And what did Putnam himself do?

MOTHER. — He was the last one upon the hill. Finding himself in great danger of being overtaken, he struck his spurs into his horse, and galloped down the rocky steep. The English dragoons dared not follow, but they fired upon him, one bullet passing through his hat.

He escaped to the next town, where he rallied more men. He could not face the enemy in open battle, but he followed them when they were leaving the town, and took fifty prisoners.

WILL. — Brave old Put !

MOTHER. — The English officer, on learning afterwards of the kind treatment these prisoners received, wrote a letter of thanks to General Putnam.

XXVI.

THE WAR AT THE SOUTH.

LIZZIE. — If I had been living a hundred years ago, I should rather have lived in one of the southern states, because the people there didn't know as much about the war as they did in the north.

WILL. — I don't say that! I should like to have been where I could help drive the red-coats out of the country.

MOTHER. — Do not imagine that the southern states were free from the horrors of war. During the years 1779 and 1780, the people at the south had dreadful times.

As the English were so unsuccessful in getting control of the middle and northern states, they determined to try their luck in Georgia.

WILL. — That was the state farthest south.

MOTHER. — And it was not so strongly defended as the others. Many of the people in Georgia and the two Carolinas were Tories.

LIZZIE. — What do you mean by Tories?

MOTHER. — The Tories were people sympathizing with the king.

16

WILL. — Then they didn't believe in the war.

MOTHER.— No; and General Clinton rightly thought that Georgia would be more willing than New England to submit. Take your maps, and see what city you should think the English would take first.

WILL. — I suppose the largest city, Savannah.

MOTHER. — General Clinton sent a large body of troops, under command of one of his colonels, to take this place. The people of Georgia were completely surprised; and Savannah fell at once into the hands of the English.

After this, General Provost arrived with more troops, and took command of all the English forces. Soon he had possession of the whole state.

LIZZIE. — O dear! Why didn't Washington send some soldiers down there?

MOTHER. — The few American troops stationed there fought desperately before they gave up. A large body of French soldiers went there too, to help them. But their general was soon wounded, so that the French were of little use at this time.

The English then marched north, and captured the largest city of South Carolina.

WILL. — That was Charleston.

MOTHER. — British troops were sent into every part of the state; and the people had to do just what the invaders said they must, or be punished.

WILL. — What! Were there no brave men there to stand up for their rights, and drive off the cowards?

MOTHER. — As I told you, there were many who sympathized with the king —

LIZZIE. — Yes — Tories!

MOTHER. — And these Tories said, "What is the use of carrying on the war any longer? America will never be free. If the colonists only do what George III. asks, he will treat them well. Besides, we cannot help ourselves."

LIZZIE. — I wish James Otis or Patrick Henry had been there to stir up the people.

WILL. — Better still if they could have had Old Put!

MOTHER. — South Carolina did not submit to British rule so easily as Georgia had done. There were many stanch patriots there, who would have died rather than give up their liberties. Besides, the English were hurting their own cause very much by treating the people unkindly. They burned houses, destroyed fields of rice and tobacco, and drove hundreds of women and children from their homes. These innocent victims wandered through the swamps half clothed and half starved.

Besides this, the English officers gave their men

leave to steal everything they could lay their hands on. All this savage treatment worked well for the Americans. Many Tories now turned patriots. " If George III. allows his officers to treat people in this way, he needn't expect South Carolina to be his colony any longer," they said.

As I told you, there were fortunately many brave men in the Carolinas, who were determined to resist the oppressions of the British. One of the most famous of these South Carolina patriots was named Marion. His father was a Huguenot.

LIZZIE. — O, I remember about the Huguenots! They came from France, and settled in South Carolina.

MOTHER. — Marion was a poor man. He worked at farming before the war. But every one who knew him respected him, for he was brave, honest, and kind-hearted. He had a great talent for drilling men into soldiers.

When he saw how the English were treating the southerners, he was very indignant, and rallied a little company of men around him, who promised to fight in case of need. He had one singular trait as an officer: he never compelled his men to stay in service. He used to say, " If a man doesn't love his country well enough to stay, he won't make a good soldier, and I don't want him."

WILL.—That made his men ashamed to run away.

MOTHER.—He rarely had a man desert him. Another singular fact about Marion was, that he had no one place for his little band of heroes to stay in. When they were not engaged in fighting, they all went home to take care of their farms and their families.

WILL.—How did they know when they were wanted?

MOTHER.—Marion had a secret signal which his men all understood; and when they heard the signal they would leave everything and hasten to their leader.

He never had many men under his command at a time; but he was a great torment to the English. Having no ammunition, and the colony being too poor to give him any, he depended on what he got from the enemy. Knowing every swamp and every forest in South Carolina, Marion and his men would secrete themselves near the English, and spring out upon them, when they supposed he was at the other end of the colony.

WILL.—You said the English were scattered all over the state. So I suppose Marion attacked small parties of the troops, instead of going into regular battles with the army.

MOTHER. — That was his constant plan. He finally became such a plague to the enemy, that they sent out large bodies of men to find him.

LIZZIE. — Why, they hunted him as they would a wild beast. Did they catch him?

MOTHER. — Many a time they would drive him to a forest or swamp, sure that they would take him back to the camp a prisoner; but to their astonishment he would disappear. So they gave him the name of the Swamp Fox.

There was a great difference between Marion and the English officers. He always treated his prisoners well, while the English would often hang a dozen American prisoners without a moment's warning.

Nothing made Marion so angry as to find his men plundering, or treating any one unkindly.

WILL. — Then the people must have liked Marion best. He didn't have to fight the English in South Carolina without any help — did he?

MOTHER. — General Gates was sent down with a large number of men. He was much needed, for Cornwallis himself was at the head of the British forces in the south.

LIZZIE. — Then I guess something was done for the Americans, for Gates was the general that gained such a victory at Saratoga, when Burgoyne had to give up.

MOTHER. — Every one expected this; but people were disappointed. General Gates fought the enemy several times, but always met with great loss. So he was finally called back, and General Greene was sent down.

WILL. — You haven't told us much about him.

MOTHER. — General Greene was second only to Washington. Indeed, Washington himself had the greatest confidence in him, saying that he was " wise, brave, and cool," three very important traits in a commander.

General Greene was much shocked at the brutal manner in which Cornwallis treated his prisoners and those people of South Carolina who showed a love of America. But from the first, he gave orders that his men should treat all kindly.

LIZZIE. — The southerners must have hated Cornwallis.

MOTHER. — The friends of George III. were decreasing rapidly; and Cornwallis saw that the English power in South Carolina was daily growing weaker.

WILL. — Wasn't General Greene glad to have the help of Marion?

MOTHER. — Yes. For some reason, Gates had taken but little notice of him; but General Greene knew his worth, and at once sent word to him that he hoped he would keep on serving his country; and he sent Marion a large number of soldiers.

General Greene divided his army into two parts, sending the larger portion to the western part of the state. His plan was to drive the English towards the coast. Soon there was a large battle at a place called Cowpens, in which the Americans lost but a few men, while the enemy lost hundreds, besides a great deal of ammunition.

There were several battles during the next year, in which the English were victorious; but they often lost so much, in men and stores, that they thought best to retreat.

At one time the Americans under General Greene retreated, and were chased by Cornwallis across North Carolina into Virginia.

WILL. — O, why didn't General Greene make a stand and face the English?

MOTHER. — For the same reason that many battles were lost by the Americans: most of them were without shoes, and were poorly clothed. Besides this, they did not have half enough to eat.

You would think that Cornwallis, with his finely drilled troops, could easily overtake our barefooted, half-starved soldiers; but it was singular that twice, when the red-coats were about to attack the rear of the army, the Americans escaped by crossing rivers, and when they were safely on the other side, a sudden rise of the streams delayed Cornwallis, so that when he got across, the Americans were miles away.

WILL. — Good! Wasn't that strange — that the water should rush to the help of the Americans?

MOTHER. — Cornwallis finally gave up the chase; and Greene, going around the English army, returned into North Carolina. The two armies had a battle here, in which the English were much crippled. After this, Greene went again into South Carolina; and by the help of Marion and other brave officers he succeeded in driving the enemy back from the interior; so that at the close of the year all the places held by Cornwallis in the south were Charleston and Savannah.

WILL. — I know what made the Americans beat so often: it was because they loved their country, and because they had pluck. That's what did it.

MOTHER. — You remind me of a story about Marion, which I will tell before we close our talk about the war in the south.

LIZZIE. — O, good! Do tell us!

MOTHER. — One day, after a severe battle, an English officer brought into Marion's camp a white flag, or flag of truce, to ask for an exchange of prisoners. After the business was over, the officer was about to leave, when Marion urged him to remain and dine. The officer, either too polite or too curious to refuse, accepted the invitation.

He looked around and saw a fire, but no other signs of a repast, and was greatly surprised when he heard Marion tell one of his men to bring in the dinner. He was still more astonished when he found that their only plates were clean pieces of bark, and all they had to eat was a quantity of sweet potatoes that had been nicely baked in the glowing ashes of the fire.

"Excuse me, General Marion," said the English officer; "but is this your usual fare?"

"Well, no, sir," answered Marion. "I am glad to say, since you are here to share my dinner, that it is better than usual."

"What!" exclaimed the English officer, as he looked about upon the sturdy men in Marion's camp, "do you mean to say that your troops are willing to put up with such rations? You must have to pay them well."

"Sir," exclaimed Marion in return, "do you suppose my men stay by me for wages merely, or for what they get to eat? We are fighting for our country, for freedom; and we shall keep on fighting as long as body and soul hold together."

The English officer could say no more. He was

so impressed by what he had seen and heard, that he gave up his commission, and went home to England. "Such men deserve their freedom," said he; "and I'll not be one to hinder them from getting it."

XXVII.

A TRAITOR.

MOTHER. — To-night I will tell you about a man whose name even is like a blot on my story — Benedict Arnold.

LIZZIE. — If he was a bad man, I hope he wasn't an American.

MOTHER. — He was one of those who hastened to join the army at Cambridge, after the battles of Lexington and Concord.

He had received a good education, and was very talented. This brought him into notice, and he soon received an important place in the army. He showed so much courage and coolness in time of danger, and understood so well the managing of an army, that Washington looked upon him as one of his best officers. But he was never a favorite. He was selfish and fond of showing his power. His greatest fault was his love of money. To get that, he often did what any high-minded man would scorn to do. He was generally in debt. Notwithstanding all this, he was so able a man that finally he became a general.

At the time of Burgoyne's surrender, Arnold received a severe wound, which unfitted him for active service for some time. And as Washington thought highly of his skill as an officer, he petitioned Congress to give him command of the forces in Philadelphia, after the English left it. But his career in that place was not pleasing to the patriots. He made intimate acquaintances with the enemies of his country. He married the daughter of a leading Tory—a beautiful and accomplished young lady.

WILL. — I don't know that he ought to be blamed for that.

MOTHER. — What was most disliked in him there, was his extravagant way of living.

WILL. — Of course *that* showed he wasn't a true patriot.

LIZZIE. — If he had been, he would have helped the poor soldiers, instead of spending so much on himself.

MOTHER. — Every one saw that he spent more than his income. He rode in an elegant coach drawn by four horses, and kept a great many servants. He gave very costly parties.

Finally people became so vexed, that the authorities of Philadelphia sent a complaint to Congress, saying they felt sure that he was spending the public money for his own use.

Congress appointed a number of army officers to look into his affairs. His money matters showed either wrong management or dishonesty, and Arnold was reprimanded.

LIZZIE. — I don't know what you mean by that.

MOTHER. — Congress told him he must behave himself or lose his place. This made Arnold very angry. He said to himself, " Here I have been working hard for the country these four years. I have often risked my life where other officers dared not go. And this is the pay I get!"

He was deeply in debt at this time. He resolved to make a desperate plunge to save himself, even if he ruined his country.

LIZZIE. — O, he wouldn't do that!

MOTHER. — You have not heard yet of West Point, so I must tell you it is on the Hudson, and was then considered one of the most important places in the country.

WILL. — Then I suppose there was a fort there.

MOTHER. — Yes ; and Washington caused it to be well supplied with cannon and ammunition, so that it would be impossible for the enemy to take it. Find it on your maps, and see if you can tell why it was such an important place.

WILL. — If the British had the Hudson, they could cut off New England from the other states.

MOTHER. — The traitor Arnold sent word to General Clinton that he would give it over to England.

LIZZIE. — O, what could make him so wicked?

WILL. — I don't see how he could bring this about.

MOTHER. — After leaving Philadelphia, he sent to Washington, asking the command of West Point. Washington gave him the place. For eighteen months Arnold secretly wrote letters to General Clinton. At last the time had come when West Point was to be given to the English. But Arnold must be sure of his money. He must get a written paper, signed by General Clinton, promising to pay over the sum at a given time. So he wrote, asking to meet some English officer of rank, who should bring the important paper. In return he would give a plan of West Point, telling how many troops were in it, and showing the easiest place of attack.

General Clinton chose young Major André for this service. André was a great favorite, kind-hearted, accomplished, brave, and handsome. One dark night he and Arnold, both disguised, met among the bushes on the banks of the Hudson. They exchanged papers, André concealing his between his stockings and the soles of his feet.

After a long talk, morning began to dawn, and Arnold was soon safely back at West Point. But

Major André was not so fortunate. On his way to the English camp, he was met by three sturdy young Americans, who were out watching the road lest English soldiers should go into the country to plunder.

One of these men, John Paulding, pointed a musket at André, commanding him to " halt ! "

The three Americans were somewhat disguised; and André's heart rejoiced, for he felt sure he was with English soldiers. Forgetting himself, he said, —

" I am a British officer. Do not stop me, for I am on very important business ! "

As he said this, he drew out an elegant gold watch. This made Paulding feel sure that he was a British officer; for gold watches were then very scarce in the colonies. So Paulding said, —

" We are Americans, and you are our prisoner ! "

Then they searched him, and found the important papers.

" Heavens ! " exclaimed Paulding, when he glanced at them; " he is a spy ! "

André tried to buy himself off.

" Let me go," he said, " and I will give you my horse and five hundred dollars."

" If you would give us five thousand dollars," answered his captors, " we would not let you stir a step."

And André was soon within prison-walls.

Lizzie. — Poor André !

Will. — Brave, honest John Paulding saved his country.

Mother. — Washington had heard nothing of the arrest. On that very day he had sent word to Arnold that Lafayette and himself would be his guests next morning.

Suspecting nothing, they were escorted up the Hudson. As they drew near the fort, Washington was greatly surprised that no military salute was fired. He was still more astonished to be informed on landing, that Arnold was away.

Soon a messenger arrived, with the papers found in André's stockings. Washington looked them over, and handed them to Lafayette, exclaiming, —

" Whom can we trust now ? "

Instantly he sent out troops to find Arnold and arrest him. But it was too late; he was already in the British camp.

Lizzie. — And Major André — what became of him?

Mother. — He was tried, found guilty, and condemned to die.

When General Clinton heard of this, he wrote to Washington, begging that his life might be spared. But Washington could not grant the request; and André died bravely as he had lived.

17

WILL. — And Arnold — the black traitor?

MOTHER. — He received a part of his money; but the English officers and soldiers all hated him.

After this he led a body of British troops into Virginia, trying to subdue that colony. But he was unsuccessful. Washington sent Lafayette to oppose him, and he was soon driven out of the state.

The longer Arnold lived, the more he was shunned; and he died in London, a despised man.

XXVIII.

VICTORY AT LAST.

MOTHER. — The war had now been going on for six years.

WILL. — Then you are going to tell us about the year 1781.

MOTHER. — Washington had had much to discourage him during the year 1780.

WILL. — Arnold had done a mean thing, to be sure; but the English hadn't made much headway.

LIZZIE. — They had been driven out of North Carolina, and had left New Jersey.

WILL. — And they didn't hold any part of the southern states but Charleston and Savannah.

MOTHER. — That is true. But you must remember that during the war business was stopped in a great measure, which made the times harder every year. As the people were earning less money than usual, they couldn't pay their taxes; so that Congress found it very difficult to get money for the soldiers. At first the soldiers didn't mind this; but after a while it became very hard to bear.

LIZZIE. — Why, yes; because if the soldiers

couldn't have their pay, they had nothing to send home to their families.

MOTHER. — The fare, too, of the men in the army was wretchedly poor. This caused many to lose their health. At one time the Pennsylvania soldiers mutinied — that is, they declared they would desert unless they could have better fare.

This troubled Washington more than anything else, for he knew the soldiers were not greatly to blame. He urged Congress to make still greater efforts to help the army.

WILL. — I don't see what Congress could do when it couldn't get money.

MOTHER. — There is no knowing what might have happened to the Americans if it had not been for a few rich men who loved their country better than their wealth. These generous patriots gave a great deal of money to Congress, because they pitied the distress of the soldiers. Besides this, France sent over a large sum. These helps were a great relief to Washington, for he had been afraid that the army would be broken up.

WILL. — Then the English would have beaten, sure !

MOTHER. — In 1781, Washington felt that some decisive steps must be taken to weaken the English army. General Clinton was still idle in New York.

WILL. — And Cornwallis was in South Carolina?

MOTHER. — He had left the Carolinas and marched into Virginia. Here he was doing great mischief, destroying all the property that came in his way. Finally, he made a stop at Yorktown, which he began to fortify. — Find it, please.

LIZZIE. — I see it. It is near Chesapeake Bay, on the York River.

WILL. — And there is James River, not far off.

MOTHER. — Just opposite Yorktown is a point of land called Gloucester. This Cornwallis also fortified.

LIZZIE. — Where was Washington at this time?

MOTHER. — He was still near New York. He had made up his mind to attack Clinton; but just then he heard the good news that a large French fleet would soon reach Chesapeake Bay.

LIZZIE. — Did he give up his plan, then, of attacking General Clinton?

MOTHER. — Yes; but he took great pains to conceal the fact. He caused a large place to be marked out for an encampment in New Jersey. Ovens were built, and fuel was piled up for the baking of bread. Even his own men thought Washington's plan was to attack New York. The day came when the supposed attack was to be made. The men were marching, as they thought, towards the city; when suddenly they were ordered to face about, and they found themselves started for the south.

Before they reached Virginia, however, Clinton guessed their object; and in order to draw back a part of the American troops, he sent the traitor Arnold into Connecticut, with a body of red-coats. Two or three towns were plundered and then burned.

WILL. — Washington was too wise to be cheated by him, I hope.

MOTHER. — He had left enough troops at West Point and other places on the Hudson to meet any immediate need; and he kept on towards Yorktown.

On his way he stopped at his home, Mount Vernon. It was the first time he had been there for six years. But, dear as the spot was to him, he felt he must not pause more than a few hours. He pushed on, and soon arrived with his army before Yorktown. Here he was made very happy by the news that the French had arrived before him, and had blocked York and James rivers.

WILL. — Good! Was Lafayette in Virginia then?

MOTHER. — Yes; and by Washington's orders he was sent to prevent Cornwallis from retreating into North Carolina.

Lafayette was soon joined by a large body of the

French soldiers.   He quickly arranged his troops
in a semicircle around the English army. Cornwallis
could . now make no retreat back into Virginia,
neither could he receive food or any kind of help
from the surrounding country.   The French fleet
prevented him from receiving aid by way of the
sea.

WILL. — Aha, Mr. Cornwallis, you got shut up
that time, like a mouse in a trap!

MOTHER. — The British army soon began to be
greatly distressed for want of food; and they had
to kill many of their horses to make the grain hold
out.

Cornwallis sent word to Clinton that he must have
help soon, or he would be obliged to give up.

WILL. — He did not have as many troops as
Washington — did he?

MOTHER. — No; the American and French troops
together numbered sixteen thousand.   Cornwallis
had but half that number.

WILL. — I can see that things began to look
pretty bright now for the Americans. Cornwallis
couldn't get away by land or sea without breaking
through the American forces.

LIZZIE. — And for once his men couldn't get
enough to eat.

MOTHER. — There was nothing left for Cornwallis

to do but to wait for help from Clinton, and to make his forts stronger.

WILL. — I hope Washington let the red-coats smell some of his powder before Clinton arrived.

MOTHER. — On the 9th of October, 1781, orders were given to bombard Cornwallis's forts. Washington himself put the match to the first gun. A furious discharge of cannon followed, and Lord Cornwallis received his first salutation. This bombardment was kept up for several days.

Cornwallis's ammunition began to fail, and he saw that he could no longer hold out. Rather than give up, he decided to try to escape by night. He hoped to break through the French troops, and make his way to join Clinton in New York.

Sixteen boats were secretly prepared. A large part of the troops had crossed the river before midnight. The remainder were about to enter the boats, when a violent storm of wind and rain arose, which scattered the boats and drove them down the river. They were brought back with difficulty. It was too near daybreak to get the remaining troops across. The army, already weakened, must not be divided. The recovered boats were used to bring back the troops that had already crossed.

Cornwallis now saw that his case was hopeless. If he kept on fighting, he would lose what brave men had not already fallen through sickness or battle. Nothing was left for him to do but to give up.

WILL. — That's just the way General Howe had to get out of Boston. Did Cornwallis lose many men?

MOTHER. — Between five and six hundred had been killed. The rest became prisoners to the Americans.

WILL. — I say, wasn't that a big victory?

LIZZIE. — And so few men killed! I am glad of that. But you didn't tell us how many *we* lost.

MOTHER. — The Americans and French together lost but about three hundred men.

I think there is nothing that better shows us Washington's greatness as a general than the fact that his most brilliant victories were gained by skilful managing, rather than by having many men killed. I have read stories of generals who have won great victories, that the world will always talk about; but I never read of any successful commander who lost fewer men than Washington.

WILL. — I wish I could have seen how the red-coats looked when they marched out of Yorktown. Did our troops see them?

MOTHER. — Our army was drawn up in two lines, each more than a mile long — the Americans on one side of the road, the French on the other; Washington, mounted on a noble horse and attended by his officers, in front of his men, and the French commander and his suite in front of theirs.

LIZZIE. — I suppose it was easy to tell which were the French, for they would have nicer uniforms.

MOTHER. — And they had a band of music playing — a luxury that our troops could never afford.

WILL. — The American soldiers didn't have on such fine clothes, of course. But O, how proud they must have looked as they stood there, waiting to see the king's troops — brave English red-coats — march out as their prisoners!

MOTHER. — Soon the British troops appeared. They were all in new uniforms; but they looked anything but soldier-like. Their drums were beating a British march; but their step was careless and irregular, their looks were sullen. How could they help it, when they saw their flags closely folded, instead of fluttering in the breeze?

As Cornwallis was sick, they were led by one of his generals, who, riding up to Washington, delivered to him his sword. In like manner, the officer of the English fleet gave up his sword to the French commander.

Then, in the name of the American people, the English army was ordered to pass into an adjoining field, where they were commanded to lay down their arms upon the ground. This vexed the red-coats so much that many of them threw down their muskets with such violence as to break them.

After this the prisoners were led back to York-town, where they were to await orders from Congress.

WILL. — I wonder what General Clinton thought when he heard the news!

MOTHER. — Five days after the surrender, General Clinton with seven thousand men arrived off the coast of Virginia. But when he heard of the fate of his comrade Cornwallis, he set sail again for New York.

LIZZIE. — And what did the people of America say?

MOTHER. — At the news of the glorious victory, great rejoicing broke forth from one end of the country to the other. Bells were rung, cannons fired, and towns illuminated everywhere. Congress set apart a day of thanksgiving, in gratitude to God, who had helped the colonies gain their independence.

LIZZIE. — And did George III. really say now that the colonies were free?

MOTHER. — It was a bitter disappointment to him to lose so much territory; and for a year or two

after the surrender of Cornwallis he was unwilling
to recognize American independence. But people
in England had become very tired of the war; and
the best men in Parliament voted that peace should
be declared. So George III. finally gave his unwilling assent.

Several men were sent from America and England
to Paris, to talk over the conditions of peace. The
principal one from this country was Franklin. It
took several months to settle upon terms that were
satisfactory to all. But in 1783, a treaty was signed.

The English soldiers were called home; and
George III. acknowledged to the world that the
UNITED STATES OF AMERICA were free and inde-
pendent.

WILL. — Hurrah for Washington!

LIZZIE. — Now that the war was over, Washington and all our tired soldiers could go home and
rest.

WILL. — They had had a hard time of it — eight
years in camp and field!

XXIX.

THE SHIP OF STATE.

MOTHER. — As I think of our country a little less than a hundred years ago, she seems to me like a great ship, in a rough and boisterous sea. As she is tossed by the stormy billows, she seems impatient to traverse the ocean, and try her speed with other great ships. I see many passengers on board, and gallant sailors ready and willing for work. But I hear them say they have no chart and no compass.

WILL. — Then they can't be safe, far away from shore.

LIZZIE. — Why don't the captain send for a chart?

MOTHER. — The ship has no captain. Many passengers think this is no matter. But the more thoughtful are anxious, and say, "We shall be wrecked, if we go to sea as we are."

WILL. — I see what you mean. The sailors are the men who want to serve their country. The chart and compass are the right kind of government.

LIZZIE. — And by the captain you mean a leader.

MOTHER. — I think you are beginning to see what our country needed. People in Europe were watching America with the greatest interest. Kings and emperors said, " The idea of so many people trying to govern themselves ! They will soon get to quarrelling with each other; then we shall see what will become of them."

But the best and wisest men everywhere hoped that America would become what the forefathers said it should — an asylum for the poor and oppressed of all lands.

LIZZIE. — If there were men wise enough to make the Declaration of Independence, I should think there would be no trouble in getting a chart for America.

MOTHER. — You are right. Three years after peace was declared, the principal men of the country met together to decide upon the best plan of government; only they didn't call it a chart, but a constitution.

They finally agreed on what would be best for the country; and all the states promised to be guided by this constitution.

WILL. — Now they wanted a leader.

MOTHER. — And whom do you think they chose ?

LIZZIE. — I guess Franklin.

MOTHER. — The people chose their first leader in 1789. Think a moment, and you will see how old Franklin was at this time.

LIZZIE. — Franklin was born in 1706. So he must

have been eighty-three years old. Of course he couldn't work for the country much longer. I am sorry, for who would make so good a leader?

Washington as first President.

WILL. — I think they chose Washington. He had been with the people so much during the war that everybody loved him.